Murder
in
Grant County

Murder in Grant County

Simon Zeller

Cedar House, Inc.
Faribault, Minnesota

© Copyright 2019 Simon Zeller
All rights reserved.

Published by Cedar House, Inc,. Faribault, Minnesota
www.cedarhouseinc.com
simon43zeller@gmail.com

Designed by Dorie McClelland, springbookdesign.com

Front cover design by Robyn Lingen, designwritestudios.com

ISBN: 978-0-9968454-3-4

Printed in the United States of America by Bookmobile

CONTENTS

PREFACE *vii*
PROLOGUE: A WORRIED CHILD *ix*

Introduction: The Court *1*

PART ONE: THE HARTMAN FAMILY 9

1   Early struggles *11*
2   Conrad *21*
3   Ada *35*
4   Tragedy *43*
5   Raymond's support *53*
6   The family next door *57*

PART TWO: THE SCHREADER FAMILY 63

7   German beginnings *65*
8   Thoughts about leaving Germany *69*
9   The journey across a nation *73*
10   The Atlantic *79*
11   Ellis Island *85*
12   Across America *89*
13   Making a home *97*
14   Traveling to Canada *101*
15   Martin and Martha's new home *111*
16   New responsibilities *123*
17   Time to learn and grow *131*

18	Duluth's challenges	*135*
19	Martin's new job	*139*
20	A new challenge	*143*
21	Foundation for an event	*147*

PART THREE: A COLLISION OF FAMILIES *151*

22	The beginning of the end	*153*
23	The plan	*163*
24	The bad check	*171*
25	A new plan	*175*
26	The search	*183*
27	The confession	*187*
28	The trial and sentence	*191*

EPILOGUE *193*

PREFACE

THE LATE 1940S AND EARLY 1950S contained my elementary school years. I frequently traveled with my parents in rural Minnesota to visit people who had no children. Without anything to read, without a radio or a television, I listened to adult conversation. Occasionally, a past murder from our neighborhood was talked about. His name was Wayne Hartman who was currently serving his sentence at the state penitentiary in Stillwater, Minnesota. He was sentenced to life, but everyone assumed he would either get out early or escape. Whenever his name was introduced into the conversation, the voices in the room would become louder and more anxious. The mere mention of the name, Wayne Hartman, made the men of Grant County and surrounding counties feel that they should have a gun at their side to protect themselves and their families. They thought that this murderer had a list of people he intended to harm or even kill. No one knew who was on this supposed "hit list." As a child, the mystery surrounding this murder grew in my mind. Now, nearly sixty-five years later, I have attempted to reconstruct and understand the happenings of that time. This book is a book of fiction based on fact. As the events encompass the 1930s and extend to the present day, they do closely resemble an accurate detail of events as much as the research was able to confirm.

This narration started with the thought that most of the information would be drawn from the two protagonists,

Wayne Hartman and Al Schreader who was the victim. Instead, it became a story of two women, the mothers of these two men. It is meant to inform us how these mothers started their early days and grew as women to take care of themselves and the men in their lives. This book is dedicated to their memory:

Ada Hartman — Martha Schreader

PROLOGUE

A WORRIED CHILD

SUNDAY, FEBRUARY 1, 1953, was a brutal and cold day in Morris, Minnesota. Dwight David Eisenhower, the hero of World War II, had just been inaugurated as the 34th president of the United States. Rocky Marciano, the world heavyweight boxing champion, also a hero, was about to deliver the hardest blow ever to the chin of Ezzard Charles. The world seemed to be at peace. Memories were still fresh for the fallen loved ones. A truce had been signed that seemed to end the Korean War. Two new countries began their march in divergent directions. South Korea positioned itself to become a democracy and similar peoples in North Korea headed themselves toward a communist dictatorship.

Grant County, Minnesota, just adjacent to Morris in Stevens County, was experiencing an extreme cold snap following a two-day blizzard that left a blanket of snow thirty inches deep. The county was paralyzed. Schools would likely be closed on Monday, farm families would make their way through the heavy white blanket to care for their vulnerable and thirsty animals, pick the eggs and milk the cows that were locked in the barns. Hard-working woodstoves in the farm houses were busy heating pails of water as fire burned aggressively in their bellies. Buckets of hot water were taken from the stove and carried to the animal shelters along paths made by the first person to reach the hungry and thirsty animals. Walking was difficult, the track was uneven and slippery, significant amounts of water were spilled before the heavy water pails reached their destination. The water containers in the barn were frozen solid, so they crackled as the hot water was spilled against the ice. On farms where the owner was forward-looking in his agricultural practice, there were water pipes installed from recently drilled wells. Those pipes were also frozen solid and were of no help when the Fahrenheit temperature reached thirty-two degrees below zero. They also had to be thawed by the hot water from the raging stove.

The Gieselman home was heated by only one very hot cooking stove. That had been the case since 1902, the year this land was settled and the house was built. In many ways, the house was old and tired. It groaned and cracked as the timbers were forced to shrink in reaction to the frigid temperature. A one-day stack of split wood sat in the dry entrance of the house. It was intended that this source of energy be close for feeding the stove. As was usually the case, the kitchen was very hot, rooms that surrounded the kitchen grew colder as their distance from the heating source grew longer. The rooms farthest away from the kitchen were the bedrooms for the children. In this weather, they were near freezing. All doors were left wide open to allow the heat to travel to the outer reaches of the home. Chamber pots, used in this very cold weather so no one had to venture outside in the night to use the outhouse, were normally frozen by morning. The vapor from one's breath was clearly visible. All the blankets and winter coats were piled on the bed for warmth and heat. Children whose beds were farthest from the kitchen huddled closely to share their warmth. It was hard to sleep since it was necessary to keep your nose above the heavy blankets enabling you to breathe. This made for ice cold noses and difficult sleep. Frost covered the windows of the house allowing light to pass through but prevented one from seeing outside. When it was time to use the facilities, each person needed to make a choice between the chamber pot or a small outhouse located about 100 feet from the kitchen door.

The outhouse had no heat. In the winter, small amounts of snow would drift through the cracks in the walls into the small building and softly cover the toilet seat. Sitting on one of those toilet holes was a bit shocking. The temperature of the board was often a negative thirty-two degrees. The process of completing one's toilet needs was finished as fast as possible. After rapidly returning to the house, the travelers usually backed up to the kitchen stove to warm themselves. However, the longer one warmed at the stove; the colder the blankets in the bedroom became. The whole process did not allow much time for relaxation and comfort.

John Gieselman knew that his son, Donnie, would not have to go to school. Donnie would be available to help with the chores and then assist in the heavy snow removal. Donnie liked the idea of missing school. He usually liked to help some, but he hoped that his dad would do most of the work. His dad, John, was worried that his nearly new DC Case tractor would not start because the oil would be thick. The tractor had a new snow bucket that was intended for days just like this. He had purchased a new tractor this past summer from Eystad Implement in the nearby town of Morris. He needed to clear the snow from his yard so his brother and a neighbor could arrive tomorrow evening in order to discuss a land transaction. Hopefully, the road to their farm from the highway would be plowed by then, as well.

Sitting in the hardwood rocker by the hot stove made John

sleepy. His bones ached. He continued to think about how he might reach some agreement on the land purchase with his neighbor, Olaf Swenson. John saw himself as a shrewd man and also somewhat of a caretaker for his younger brother who would also be part of the land purchase. Knowing his brother's manipulations, he was feeling nervous and unsure of himself. It seemed as if Olaf was certain he could get sixty-five dollars per acre from someone, but John was not so sure. He wanted the land with his brother for forty-five dollars an acre, a total of one thousand eight hundred dollars which he felt was a fair price since the land was only good for pasture. Olaf and his wife, Mildred, would be coming tomorrow evening for coffee, a piece of pie and debate. For that to happen, John needed the county snowplow to clear the road of the snow that blocked his driveway. If all went well, the next evening the Swanson's would be able to come for the planned visit.

Fortunately, between the County snowplow and John's hard work moving the snow in the yard, the Swensons were able to arrive to discuss this serious land transaction. Without revealing how he felt, Olaf knew that he could no longer raise any more cattle for farming because he was seventy-six years old and his health was declining. He seriously hoped that he could reach an agreement with John and his brother. With the sale of the land, he would have enough money to retire and buy the old Anderson place in Alberta.

Old man Anderson had died this past year, and his house was sitting empty. Mrs. Anderson moved in with her daughter in Herman. She had an elderly cousin in town by the name of George Torkelson. George's wife died sixteen years ago, and he rejoiced at the possibility of spending time with his cousin, Mrs. Anderson, whom he liked very much. He did worry that some townsfolk may gossip because he was spending time with a single woman even if she were his cousin.

The drifting snow had slowed and the moon was full. The Swenson's made the one-and-a-half- mile journey to meet with John and his brother, Francis. Old man Swenson's hip was sore that evening. He complained about how hard it was to throw hay from the barn loft. However, in the same breath, he reminded the brothers that the 40 acres of land were very profitable and his price was reasonable.

Coffee was served with cream on the side. John's wife, Alma, had baked a lemon cream pie for the occasion. The land discussions began almost immediately. After some debate, an agreement was reached with both the buyer and the seller complaining about the outcome. As the evening discussion closed, the name of Wayne Hartman was mentioned. It seems that someone had heard that he might be released from prison. The ladies at the local Lutheran Church during a guild meeting wondered whether there were other people in Grant County who may have to fear for their lives. After all, many said that the killer had no remorse. They were sure he had other enemies. For years the Hartman name sparked fear in the communities of Elbow Lake and Herman.

During the visit, eight-year-old Donnie was trying to go to sleep in his cold bed. He listened intensely to the low conversations in the next room. He was hoping that his father would buy the forty acres of pasture from the Swenson's. He loved to explore the out-of-doors and the small wooded areas. There was a small pond in the center that seemed to have thousands of frogs every summer. He loved to catch them. His pulse quickened as he could hear the vague voices of four adults discussing a dangerous man. The conversation made him feel uncomfortable and made it hard to sleep.

The first day of school after a large snowstorm was a lot of fun. It meant making snow forts, sliding on hills and making caves in the deep snow during recess. He woke early to eat his oatmeal and talk to his mother. He loved that time of day. She was always encouraging and optimistic with her affectionate little boy.

Donny said, "I listened to you talking last night. It made me afraid. Is there someone nearby who might hurt us?"

He wanted to know if he should be frightened for himself and others he might know.

"Does this man kill people?" He asked.

"My dear son, no one is going to hurt us. Don't be afraid. Do you mean the bad man who hurt someone that we were talking about last night with the Swensons?"

"Yes, I heard you talking about him getting out of jail and coming back to hurt people."

Again, Mother said, "Don't be afraid, no one will hurt us."

"Oh look. The Hoglund's are driving toward the house to pick you up for school. You don't want to keep them waiting. Do you have everything?"

"Yes. I have all my homework and my lunch. See you after school. I love you, Mom."

Going to school meant that the neighboring Catholic families used their cars to take children to St. Mary's school in Morris. There was no school bus to take kids to the Catholic school. Usually, one family took responsibility for two other families to provide transportation on the short 4-mile drive to school.

Donny put on his coat and hat and ran to the car to get in with the two Hoglund sisters. They didn't say much to him as they were three and four years older. He remembered that when he was smaller they would take his hat and then laugh.

A Worried Child

Arriving at school, eight-year-old Donnie immediately ran to a small gymnasium. Other children had arrived, and they were playing noisely. They would be going to daily mass in a few minutes. Father Fearon would put on his fancy vestments for the celebration. Donny sometimes thought that he looked a bit like a big bug. He hoped thinking about Father that way was not a mortal sin. Arriving in the gym, he immediately ran to a girl in his class. He liked her very much, and they played many times. They never fought because she was always right. She always made him feel good, and he liked her for that. She could really run fast, and he was sure that she knew more things than any other kid.

"Karen, is there someone in town who might hurt us or our parents?"

Karen said, "Don't be silly, our parents will protect us." Karen seemed to be thinking about something else. Donnie was not sure she was listening to him.

"Donny, how do you like my new Buster Brown shoes?"

Just before the big storm started, Karen and her mother went to the Penny's store shopping. They purchased the shoes from Donnie's aunt, Myrtle. Myrtle had worked at the store for nearly twenty years. The tragedy that struck her life in 1939 changed everything. She never married after Wayne Hartman killed her fiancé, Al Schreader.

Karen always thought that this nice lady would be a fun mother. In her mind, she wanted to know if Myrtle had children that she had not met. Perhaps they were older and lived somewhere else.

They lined up in the gym and Donnie said a little extra prayer because he was not sure that he could trust Karen's interpretation of the situation.

As was usual for young children, the mass seemed very long.

Sometimes they fussed and teased, but Sr. Agatha was always watching. Her stern face and short ruler let everyone know that praying was probably better than talking and giggling. During the Mass, Donnie could not help but think about the bad man he heard the adults talking about last night. He wondered just what he was like, and what he had done to make people so worried about his return.

INTRODUCTION

THE COURT

June 29, 1939, was another hot day in Elbow Lake Minnesota. The temperature had reached nearly one-hundred degrees over the last five days. The weatherman from WDAY Fargo North Dakota predicted at least two more weeks of abnormally hot weather. Animals required continuous watering, the local supply of ice was rapidly disappearing. The heat penetrated everything. People slept on top of their mattresses. Many times they shed all their nighttime clothing. Small fans ran everywhere.

Judge Samuel A. Flaherty was awakening from another fitful night. His neck was clammy and wet. He could not find any spot that gave his body some relief from the temperature. At 5:30 AM sleep left him for the last time that night. The outside temperature had dropped only to eighty-four degrees while the inside temperature hovered near ninety. His wife, Mildred, was already on the front porch looking for relief. She held her cup of coffee while Sam poured one for himself. As he was pouring his cup, he thought that it was a bit ridiculous to drink hot liquid with an already overheated body. He tried hard to think of a time when the temperature provided so much misery.

Sam and Mildred had been married for thirty-five years, so Mildred knew Sam's mind very well. Today he was uncomfortable beyond the penetrating heat. This was the day he would render a judgment in the courtroom that would alter a life forever. He was always more fretful and anxious on those days. This morning Mildred would allow Sam to sit quietly and contemplate what he would soon have to do without being distracted by conversation. The sentencing of Wayne Hartman for the murder of Al Schreader had left Sam unsettled and contemplative. He knew that everyone in the area had been riveted to the details of the case as it was argued in court. Events like this murder did not happen in this rural, friendly part of Minnesota. Sam understood that folks were anxious to hear his ruling in the case.

Sam was completing his twelfth year as a county judge. The community of Elbow Lake in Grant County was small. The whole County had only about 2800 souls. Directly or indirectly Judge Flaherty touched the lives of everyone in the County. Everyone knew him and referred to him as "His Honor." It was a lonely life being so separated from the people that he met on the street each day. It was strange and uncomfortable to be addressed so formally when he really only wanted to be a friend. This loneliness along with this deep sense of responsibility could only be shared with Mildred. More often than not Sam overwhelmed Mildred with his innermost thoughts about his burden of responsibility which made him feel so lonely. There were times that all Mildred could do was to hold his worries at a distance. She was able to attend social gatherings and share gossip with her neighbors. She had learned to get her friends and neighbors to think of her as someone who did not know any of the goings-on that her husband was burdened with every day. For Sam, the tone of conversations changed as he tried to join in with neighborhood men visiting on a range of rural topics. With the authority invested in him, lives were changed with the sound of a thud from a wooden hammer. As time passed in his judgeship, Sam wanted to shrink from his responsibility. As a boy he dreamed of being important, a judgeship seemed to offer a status beyond anything his father or grandfather had ever achieved for themselves. The lofty position of a local judge initially offered no hint of the loneliness that would follow. He knew that his wife Mildred and their three children had missed many rewarding relationships as a result of the community's respect for him and that tinge of fear that he could deliver frightening judgments that deeply affected their lives.

Noticing that his coffee cup was nearly empty, Sam rose from his chair in his loose-fitting flannel pajamas, and got another cup of coffee. With a full cup in hand he opened the screen door to the porch and picked up the Minneapolis Star Tribune. Sitting in his wooden rocker, he read the headlines. Other sections of the paper would be examined later in the day while he sat by a large fan in his office during court recess.

That day, the headlines noted that King George the sixth and Elizabeth were guests at the White House visiting President Franklin Delano Roosevelt and his wife Eleanor. They were the first King and Queen to be guests of an American president. Although war was near, the article noted that the Royal couple would be eating their first hot dogs. Also, on the front page, the newspaper noted that the New York Yankees had just held a ceremony that filled Yankee Stadium in honor of the great baseball player, Lou Gehrig. Although his death was near, he said, "Today, I feel like the luckiest man alive." His passing would leave the disease that killed him with his name, Lou Gehrig's Disease. Turning to the sports page, Sam noted that a black American with the name of Joe Lewis had just won the World Heavyweight Boxing Championship. He won in a four-round knockout of Tony Galent at Madison Square Garden.

Reading these articles provided Sam with temporary relief from the burden he was about to face.

After finishing his second cup of coffee, Sam left the porch and headed for their hot bedroom to put on wool slacks and a white shirt with a drawn tie. He wore his matching wool suit coat for the two-block walk to the courthouse. He exchanged almost no words with Mildred, only to say, "Goodbye, I hope to be home for lunch."

Today Judge Samuel A. Flaherty would have the sole responsibility of sentencing Lowell Wayne Hartman to life in prison at the Minnesota State penitentiary in Stillwater, Minnesota. The Minnesota judicial system did not allow a death sentence to be imposed on anyone convicted of murder. It only allowed the judge to confine the individual and remove all of his civil rights for the remainder of his life.

Somehow Sam felt that he was condemning this man to live like a caged animal without rights or privileges. He tried hard to drive these thoughts from his mind. He continually thought about how he would feel if he were on the receiving end of a similar judgment. He could not imagine a worse feeling. Taking away the rights of another was a responsibility he yearned to have removed from his stooped shoulders. It was now 6:00 AM. The sentencing would be in handed down in three hours which was time enough for the weight of his decision to grow heavier upon him.

While he slowly walked up Main Street, his right side was already becoming uncomfortably warm from the heat of the rising Sun. He gazed at the courthouse in front of him where he would have to represent the best interests of the local citizenry. The structure was built in 1905, thirty-five years ago. It had changed very little as the city began to grow around it.

Arriving at the front steps of the building, Sam turned

around and looked to the south end of Main Street which was bordered by Round Lake. Little did he know that in 1972 it would undergo a name change to Lake Flekkefjord in honor of a sister village in Norway. Only a few automobiles lined the main street during this early morning. Horses were no longer permitted on Main Street as a result of a city ordinance passed nearly ten years earlier.

The courthouse was a red brick structure of two stories. It stood rather grand towering over the small buildings on either side. Walking from the south, it appeared rather majestic and formal for its time. Moving up the sidewalk and up the steps usually made visitors feel that they were in the presence of something that was larger than themselves and certainly more important. Two large wooden doors each with a large pane of frosted glass greeted visitors and suggested that they should remain humble while entering. Signs inside the door of the main corridor directed visitors to the second floor for the court and all activities associated with it. County offices were on the first floor to the right. The first floor contained a county jail with two cells. Today only one of the cells contained a prisoner. The hallways and floors were lined with polished decorative wood. Like most court houses, the floors crunched and squeaked as people moved from room to room. The court room itself was built to resemble courtrooms throughout the United States. This courtroom had places for twenty-five observers and county officials.

The building was empty except for the inhabitant of one of the two jail cells. There was no around-the-clock attendant to rescue an inmate should a fire occur. Everyone knew that if you were unlucky enough to be a resident of the jail during a nighttime fire, you would simply be cooked as the flames advanced. To date, all past residents of the County jail considered themselves lucky since no such catastrophe had occurred.

At 7:00 AM people began to arrive. First to arrive was the janitor followed by the clerical staff and finally by County officials. It was during these times that Sam enjoyed greeting all those present by their first name. With each greeting, those addressed responded differentially, "Good morning, Judge."

For the past eighty-five days as the morning sun rose to her back, sat a nicely dressed attractive woman in her mid-forties. She sat on a wooden bench along the sidewalk that approached the Court House. Most people entering the building during that time knew that she was Ada Hartman and that she would be asking the jailer if she could see her son. The sheriff recognized the situation as being harmless and allowed for daily visits. Early arrivals greeted her as a person whose heart had been broken. She always softly returned an accepting smile. She had come from a family of status and means and was known and respected by those who passed her sitting on the bench.

In her early days, she had taught at a local rural school where some of the courthouse arrivals had been her students. They knew her as a woman of style who seemed to nurture and love them as she taught them their lessons. She had been a popular teacher. She had come to this community from central Iowa for her teaching job. She was attracted to Elbow Lake because her brother, Raymond Teft, lived there with his wife. Since she was new to the area she had initially moved in with her newly married brother, Raymond, who was a local farmer.

Today was an especially sorrowful day because she would hear Judge Flarherty sentence her son, Wayne, to life in prison at the State Penitentiary in Stillwater for the murder of Aloysius Schreader. He had already pled guilty to the charge of murder in the 1st degree. She did not doubt his guilt.

As the nine o'clock hour approached, she gracefully stood up and walked toward the large wooden doors. She ascended to the second floor and entered the courtroom. The room was full but almost immediately people moved themselves together so that she would have a clear view of her son.

Minutes before Judge Sam Flaherty was to enter the packed courtroom, an unknown lady attempted to enter. No one seemed to know her as heads turned to note her late arrival. Since there was no seating available, the Clerk of Court informed her that she would have to leave. As she was being escorted from the courtroom, she whispered in the court officer's ear. He immediately stopped and turned into the courtroom. He asked the nearest male for his seat and motioned for this unknown woman to be seated. Most everyone in the room turned in an effort to see what was disturbing the order in the room. The woman graciously thanked the officer. She offered no knowing smile to anyone.

Recognizing her late arrival and her disruption, Sam asked, "Would the lady who just entered this court please be recognized by the Court and state her full name and her purpose for being here today?"

Without expression, the lady rose to speak. "My name is Martha Schreader, I am the mother of Aloysius Schreader. My son was the victim of the man who is about to be sentenced."

The courtroom filled with a deafening silence. Martha Schreader offered no expression. The court officials were then identified for their roles and took their seats. The door to the right of the Judge slowly opened revealing first the deputy and then a quiet, harmless looking man, Lowell Wayne Hartman. He was led to the defendant's table. With no further comment, Mr. Hartman was asked to plea.

Sam asked, "How do you plea to the murder of Aloysius Schreader on the date of April 1, 1939?"

Wayne Hartman said, "Guilty."

The defendant showed no remorse and only little interest in the happenings inside the courtroom. Without speaking, Sam waited as time passed recognizing that this man was indeed an unusual perpetrator. The facts of the case were evident but the strangeness of the man at the defendant's table was not obviously understandable.

Perhaps by exploring the history of each of these families, one can gain an understanding of the two mothers whose sons became fatally linked on April 1, 1939.

PART ONE

THE HARTMAN FAMILY

CHAPTER 1

EARLY STRUGGLES

ONE MORNING IN THE EARLY 1840S, Henry and Elizabeth Teft sat in an unkept and disheveled one room miner's shack. They had lived in the shack for nearly sixteen years. Their now fourteen-year-old son, Conrad, was still asleep on his cot above the main floor. The shack was scarred and had been repaired many times from heavy use. Assorted mixtures of smells from rancid food, burnt wood and unwashed clothing were everywhere.

A small container of water was beginning to boil for tea and would later be used for cooking a breakfast potato. There were no smiles on Henry and Elizabeth's faces which were drawn and tired. They had fought the previous evening over Henry's heavy drinking and Elizabeth's nagging responses. The fight lasted late into the evening until Henry fell asleep in a drunken stupor. The couple was still feeling tension this morning from the previous evening. Conrad tried to lay still on his small cot fearing that if he made noise his father would again begin a new quarrel with his mother.

As the sun arose in the East, ribbons of light made colorful patterns over the North Sea. The colors reflected against the bright sky and deep blue water. At a glance the world seemed full of optimism. The sounds of the saltwater birds announced the dawn to those still deep in sleep. The apparent optimism and sunshine were always discredited every day by the crush of extreme poverty for those who struggle for survival and dignity in this deprived place.

The smells of rotten food and foreboding sweat penetrated every space in this tiny structure. Henry, a "Geordie" had worked in the coal mines for over fifteen years. He started his labor at the age of thirteen to help his mother survive after the death of her husband and his father in a terrible mining accident. In the area surrounding Newcastle England, mining deaths were common. To survive after the mining accident, his mother took in wash and cleaned houses of the community's middle-class. This was done as long as Henry could remember.

At an early age, Henry married Elizabeth who was a child herself. Their only child, Conrad, was born just two months after her fourteenth birthday. She now, like all of her neighbors, lived as a slave in these dozens of unkept miners' shacks in this very crowded community. Miners' wages were kept low so there was no real possibility of moving beyond this hardship. The wages were just high enough to cover a small rent, buy food from the company store and consume alcohol whenever possible.

There was no hint of comfort or recreation. All monies available after rent and food were paid were usually spent at the local pub. Henry drank heavily every evening often passing out on a thin blanket laid on the floor in the corner of the little house. Elizabeth's only relief from this despair was an occasional conversation with another woman in a situation almost identical to her own.

Each day of a miner's life was filled with fear and worry that this may be their last. Mining accidents were common. Everyone had lost at least one person that they were dependent upon for this desperate survival. In addition to Henry's alcohol consumption, some believed that Elizabeth had gone "crazy" and could no longer stand the stress of this life worrying each day that her survival as well as that of her son could be lost if Henry were killed in an accident.

Elizabeth and Henry sat near each other staring into an abyss with unfocused eyes. Suddenly the earth shook. Kettles hanging on the wall banged and clanged as they wobbled and swayed. Candles toppled, spilling their wax and starting small fires. The tiny shack squeaked and shook. Henry's tired look changed instantly to an expression of tension and fear. Silence covered the tiny village like a blanket. Everyone knew what it happened.

The mine had exploded.

The magnitude of the blast let everyone know that this was probably the largest explosion heard in many years. Henry and Elizabeth instantly changed and sat in an intense rigidity knowing that their help and emotional support would be needed by their neighbors and friends. It was not clear to them who would soon be identified among the missing. They were certain that they would know almost all of the people working underground. They knew that as their friends were dragged from the mine into the morning air, many of them would be dead.

They each envisioned an often-repeated scene of people gathering near the mineshaft opening, screaming and weeping. This would probably happen within minutes. All grievances and troubles would quickly be forgotten in an effort to provide some form of comfort to those families who would soon be burying their dead.

Routinely, Father Edwards would be one of the early arrivals at these disasters. He quickly offered condolences and a brief conversation with anyone near who might know any of those who had been lost. If a body was brought to the surface, he administered the sacrament of Extreme Unction. He would place oil on his thumb and make the sign of the cross on the decedent's coal dusted forehead while reciting certain prayers for the dead. The scene, although known and understood by members of the mining community was dreaded and filled with terror.

The mine owners usually arrived early to offer many condolences. Despite their sympathies, the miners' families felt that the mine owner's concern was simply for a lack of labor and potential lost profits. Most often mining company gave the widow a bag of fruit, vegetables and several eggs as a final gesture for the sacrifice of her husband. Finally, with some contrived concern they offered the widow and children the shack in which they were living for another two weeks without any rent requirement. Some accepted this as an act of kindness and were grateful. Others withdrew in tears knowing that shortly they would be evicted and even more extreme poverty follow.

Children, usually little boys, were left to forage for food and were eventually invited to become mine workers themselves. Little girls were exploited in other ways. Elizabeth had grown through these terrible times without protection. Some said that during these years, demons had taken her soul. Today her usual expression was one of vigilant eyes ever watchful for potential danger and ready for a quick response. Although she could speak and carry a conversation, she never had been allowed to read or write. Families with the most dramatic losses often disappeared after being evicted and were lost forever. No one ever learned what became of them.

Seventeen miners died that day. Some families lost a husband and father while others lost a husband and several sons who were also working in the mine. It was an often-repeated tragedy for people dependent on mining for their livelihood.

Mine owners were active in supporting local churches. Losing a day of work was something to be avoided. The mines had to operate. The local clergy recognized this problem and complied with the request of the mine owners to hold all funerals on Sundays. The good pastor always received a bit of extra compensation from the mine owners and executives on the designated day of the funerals for acquiescing to their wishes.

This disaster hit Henry extra hard. He knew all the dead men and was a close drinking friend to four. It was with these four men that Henry was able to express the deep sadness of his life's failures. Without his friends to share his feelings, his pain grew. As the hurt and loneliness increased, he began to direct more anger toward Elizabeth. His threatening behavior escalated to more severe beatings. As the abuse intensified, Elizabeth's contact with any reality lessened. As he watched, Elizabeth grew more fragile and would retreat into her own mind for extended periods. As Elizabeth retreated into madness, Henry's own frailties began to be exposed with more regularity. He could no longer sleep. The skin on his feet began to loosen and his head ached constantly. He had stripped Elizabeth of all her tender strengths so that she could no longer offer him any kindness or emotional support.

Henry, in his drunken stupors, began to think of how he might get rid of Elizabeth. He began to think of her as his only source of problems. If she were gone from his life, all his problems would disappear. He had heard that other minors were able to shed the burden of marriage with the help of the mine owners. Although the Catholic Church offered no words of encouragement for him to follow this path, his mind was made up. He would go to the mine owners' office tomorrow.

Appearing confident, he told them, "Elizabeth is out of control. She accuses me of crazy things and screams and hollers."

Although his accusations contained some truth, he was not thinking of a solution for Elizabeth and their marriage. He was only focused on himself. The mine owners had solved problems like this before because they were always interested in the success of the mine. Keeping their workers productive was paramount. Removing Elizabeth but yet keeping their son, Conrad, offered multiple rewards. They would not only gain a happy worker but would soon have another miner in Conrad. This seemed like a very reasonable direction in which to proceed. There would be two miners in the shack rather than just one. Henry, like many other minors before him, needed to blame someone for his path to nowhere. Newcastle England was a gender graveyard.

The mine owners always seemed sympathetic and encouraged the miners into thinking they were essential in order for them to gain a better future. They eagerly helped Henry blame Elizabeth for his frustration with his life rather than the miserable conditions into which the mine had thrust him. The owner of the mine, after sharing his sympathies for Henry's problems, indicated he would talk to a friend at the Wilcox Asylum. Wilcox was formally considered a treatment center for people who were suffering mental illness. People could be sent there under a vague pretense of being mentally unfit. Few people who became patients ever returned to see their homes and family again. In many cases, the patient's only real fault was interfering with the function of the mine workers.

The owner suggested to Henry that he should appreciate the work being done to help him get rid of this most disagreeable woman who was the cause of his many problems. With a broad smile, Henry thanked the mine owner.

The owner said, "I will let you know on the day before the staff from Wilcox is to arrive to take Elizabeth."

Several days passed before two men wearing white coats left Wilcox with a small four wheeled buggy and a horse. The buggy contained a box that was attached to its platform which was four feet by four feet and six feet high. It had a small door in the front and two thin openings in its top to allow for air and light.

It was nearly 9:00 AM on this Wednesday morning when Conrad began to awaken after a fitful night of sleep. His parents had argued late into the night and ended only when Henry had beaten Elizabeth unconscious. As he swung his legs to the floor, he looked out the window to see an unusual appearing buggy approaching.

Neighbors stood in their doorways and watched the carriage pass. They all suspected that Henry had gone to the mine owners to have something done about Elizabeth. As the men approached the shack, the buggy started to slow. It gently stopped in front of Henry and Elizabeth's house. The man who was accompanying the driver slowly got down from the carriage and went to the door and softly knocked.

He saw the man come to the door and knock. He heard his mother go to the door and open it. "What do you want?" she said.

They answered, "Please come with us. We're here to help you."

She screamed and fell back into the tiny shack. They quickly grabbed her arms and put a tight cloth over her mouth. As they dragged her across the small room, they did not seem to care that she was being hurt. Conrad was frightened and tried to make the men let his mother go. They pushed him to the floor and continued to drag Elizabeth from the house. They tightened the gag on her mouth to attempt to stop her screams.

"NO! NO! NO!" She yelled through the gag.

Although the neighborhood was already alarmed, the attendants from Wilcox made every effort to quell Elizabeth's screams so as not to cause more distress. Elizabeth was quickly lifted into the small box on the buggy for delivery to the asylum.

Conrad briefly chased the buggy carrying his mother until the driver began to aggressively thrash him with his whip. Falling on his face, he cried in the middle of the dirt road. Margaret, the lady in the next shack who was his mother's friend, ran into the road and took him into her arms. Conrad wept and cried uncontrollably. Margaret held him to her breast and tried to reassure him that his mother would soon return.

The tiny shack was quiet as Conrad walked sadly into it. Even a brief loss of his mother's presence was totally unimaginable for the soon to be fourteen-year-old boy.

On the one-hour ride to the asylum, Elizabeth fought against her restraints and hit the sides of the box with her feet and head. The buggy arrived at the asylum where two more attendants were waiting. With three men of great strength in place, she was carried to a small room with a cot and latrine. She was now exhausted from fighting the ropes and cords wrapped around her wrists and ankles. She was left in the room without food or water with her bindings still in place for one day.

The next day, the attendants came and removed the ropes and her clothing. She was placed in a large tub of water for cleaning because she had been lying in her own waste. She was allowed to eat a small amount of food and then was wrapped tightly in a wet sheet. As the sheet dried it grew tighter. Her body felt as if it was being crushed.

This was a therapy that was considered useful in relieving the demons that had taken control of her soul. She remained in the sheet for two days, again soiling her body. This was followed by other therapies considered to be effective. She was placed in nearly freezing water for five minutes every fifteen minutes over six hours.

After this therapy, she was returned to her small cell. As she gained some strength after being allowed to rest, she again became resistant. They decided to use bloodletting in an effort to rid her body of the demons which seemed to possess her. However, this therapy seemed to be ineffective in treating her, so, as a last resort, the clinical staff decided that there must be too much pressure on her brain. They decided to open a small hole four inches above her left ear. There was no sedation for this treatment effort.

Shortly after draining her brain of fluid, a severe infection wracked her body and within hours she fell unconscious. Her death occurred one day later. She was twenty-seven years old.

No one was informed of her death and her body was taken to a potter's field just adjacent to the asylum.

CHAPTER 2

CONRAD

Conrad would soon be turning fourteen. The mine owners had decided that he would be joining the "Goergies" to live nearly half the rest of his life beneath the earth. Although most young miners did survive the mining experience, they would be facing an early and agonizing death from assorted lung diseases related to the overexposure to coal dust. The experience was nearly without exception.

Conrad watched and listened knowing that his turn would be coming in days. He thought about his mother and wondered how she was doing and when she would return. His father only told him to shut up when he asked about his mother.

One evening, as it happened so many times before, his father staggered into the shack in a state of intoxication. Henry clung to the doorframe as he laid his body down on the dirty blanket in the corner. Conrad watched with disinterest. The scene was not new. This time the evening passed as the groans grew louder. Henry was unable to sleep. His breathing was deep and not rhythmic. Conrad remained indifferent. Henry's body began to shake and eventually convulsed, hitting his head hard on the floor and banging his arms and legs against the walls.

With the suddenness of a bolt of lightning, Henry's body lay limp. His head was drawn back, his mouth remained open as his eyes stared into eternity. Conrad knew that somehow this was different. Slowly he began to realize that his father was dead.

Although one's father's death can occur only once, it is his final action. He is leaving his children forever. Conrad was familiar with this type of loneliness throughout his lifetime. This new loneliness felt a bit different but did not produce any despair. Conrad remained in the small dirty room with his dead father throughout the night. There was no one to tell.

He eventually fell asleep and was awakened by the rattling of the door. A man came to remind Henry that he was late for work. Conrad silently pointed to the corner. With little emotion, the uninvited intruder and Conrad agreed that Henry's body should be removed shortly. The man from the mine immediately informed the Sheriff and the local undertaker of Henry's death.

The undertaker came with a cheap horse-drawn hearse that contained a wooden box about the size of a man. The undertaker and his helper picked up Henry's body and put it in the box. Overnight Henry's body had stiffened, so they were unable to shut the box. Henry's knees and his head could be seen at a distance sticking out from the box on the buggy.

Without ceremony or goodbye, Conrad was alone. He began to search the tiny house for bits of food. He knew how to compete with rats for leftovers. Later in the day, a man came from the mine to tell him that if he wished he could stay in the shack and that he should report to the mine office tomorrow. No mention was made of his deceased father. Nothing was said about a burial service or a grave. Conrad thought for a moment, where was his mother? The man from the mine had no idea what had happened to her.

With nothing else to do, Conrad arose early and walked through the village of small one room shacks. The sun was beginning to rise, birds are singing, rats were scurrying about looking for safety. Most of the men had already gone to the mine. Children were not yet awake as disheveled mothers stood in doorways. Somehow all these women reminded Conrad of his mother. His memory grew stronger and sadness began to fill his soul. He had not seen her for over a year.

Arriving at the small wooden office near the mine shaft opening, Conrad entered the building to notice a man sitting at a desk with a white shirt and arm garters. The man clearly knew that someone had entered the room but remained looking at the papers in front of him with half glasses. Finally, with an annoyed expression the man looked up and harshly said, "What you want?"

Conrad responded, "I am here to go to work."

Without comment, the clerk walked into the back room leaving Conrad standing in front of the desk for nearly one-half hour.

Returning to the small waiting room, the clerk said, "Mr. Eastwick wants you to go to the docks and unload a ship coming from America."

Although Conrad had lived near this harbor for nearly fifteen years, he had never visited it.

"When you get to the water, ask for Mr. Bowles. He will tell you what to do."

After leaving the small miner's office as he walked toward the water, Conrad noticed that there were noisy seagulls everywhere and smells began to change. He walked toward the man who seemed to be giving instructions.

The man looked down at Conrad and said, "Are you here to help?"

Conrad nodded in the affirmative. The man said, "This ship is loaded with cotton for the Mills, help that man over there."

As Conrad walked over to the man, he noticed large letters on the side of the ship. He could not read but did know the alphabet. The letters read R-I-C-H-M-O-N-D. The year was 1862. This ship was loaded with cotton held in large bundles and stamped in large letters, CSA.

In the Confederate States of America, this ship was called a blockade runner. To support the Confederacy in their War effort, cotton was shipped to ports in Europe on ships which had to evade the Northern blockade of the South.

After the cotton was unloaded it would be loaded with guns and ammunition for the rebels of the Confederate states. It would return to the South by running a union blockade near Charleston Harbor in order to provide munitions for the soldiers of the South.

The boss's order intended that Conrad would stay with the ship to finish the unloading and reloading. Afterwards, he would then be assigned to a team to work in the mine.

The process of unloading and reloading the ship would take in excess of one week. Conrad had no friends in his harsh life. Other parents kept their children away from this family with an alcoholic father and a "deranged" mother.

An immediate attraction and friendship developed between the ship's Captain's butler and Conrad. Conrad had never seen a child with such dark skin before. The boy was a slave. Conrad had no understanding of the turmoil in the world. He did know that he did not want to be separated from this boy - the only friend he had ever had. The boy's name was Rufus. They talked and decided that Conrad would hide in the ship and sail with his new friend. They had no idea how this would change their lives. There was something in Conrad's instinct that told him that getting away from the mines would likely be a very good thing. The pact was struck and a hiding place was found for the stowaway aboard the ship. The journey would last at least two weeks.

The hiding place was small and allowed for almost no comfort or light. Rufus would bring small amounts of food and water when an opportunity arose. On the morning of departure, Conrad had already inserted himself through the small opening into the hideaway. He could hear the hissing of the boilers and the turning of the screw. The ship slowly rubbed against the dock and made its way into the North Sea for the trip to America. This was the first time Conrad had ever experienced the rocking of waves. His stomach immediately became upset. However, through sheer force of will, he was able to keep his food in his stomach.

The boys were sure that the adventure would be completed without incident. Although the ship was filled with the noise of sailors shouting, water splashing and engines chugging, a new noise caught Conrad's ear.

He recognized the noises as screams coming from his friend Rufus, "NO NO NO!"

He could hear hard footsteps drawing close. The small door to the hiding place flew open. There stood the angry Captain and the First Mate holding each of Rufus's arms. He was crying.

Conrad was pulled through the tiny opening and forced to stand. He had no words. If this situation were not so tense, he would've noticed that his body hurt everywhere. One week without moving causes many problems.

The captain softened his grip on Rufus because there was no place to run. Conrad stood as stiff as a stone.

The captain said, "Who is this boy, what is he doing here? He is too young to execute and furthermore, he is white so he has certain rights to life. Rufus, on the other hand, is my property. I can do what I want with him. I no longer feel he deserves my trust. Tie him to the mainmast while I decide what to do with him."

Conrad did not understand any of this. But he was sure that the situation would have a bad outcome.

The Captain grabbed each boy and slammed each to the floor. Pointing to Conrad he said, "throw him into the brig."

He then stared at Rufus and dragged him from the floor by the arm. He again threw him to the deck. The boy's eyes were filled with fear. Pointing to two unoccupied sailors, he ordered them to tie the boy firmly to the mainmast. Rufus did not struggle and accepted his punishment as a passing thing.

As the days passed, Conrad received small amounts of water. Rufus received nothing but scorn. As the captain's anger subsided, he removed Conrad from the brig to assist the sailors with their sailing duties. Rufus was left tied to the pole without food or water. His body began to sag and put strain on the ropes. Conrad passed the dying boy many times each day, but could do nothing. Eventually the body of Rufus hung limp on the pole.

One day at high noon the boy's body was cut free and cast into the ocean without ceremony. Conrad secretly wept and looked away with fear and despair. He had no understanding of why this had just happened. His life was filled with loss and cruelty. "Is this all I can ever expect?" He wondered.

As the days passed at sea, Conrad wondered if this journey would ever end. After several days had passed since Rufus's body was thrown into the sea, Conrad overheard the sailors talking about a subject or perhaps a place by the name of Charleston. Again, he had no idea what that meant.

Several days later, he saw buildings in the distance which were built along the seashore. It reminded him of the English cities that he had just left seventeen days ago. As they entered the harbor, Conrad noticed a brick structure on his right, it was a building with cannons covered with bricks and debris. It looked as if it had been destroyed.

A sailor said, "That building was full of Yankees, we destroyed it. Damn Yankees!"

For Conrad, the remarks had no meaning. The ship slowed to a halt near one of the open piers. It was strapped into place and a plank was set up from the ship to the dock.

Captain Pickering held Conrad's arm tightly and walked to the dock. He explained to an official what had just happened. He released the boy to the dock foreman to go into the city of Charleston. The dock manager decided to place Conrad in the city jail.

He was the only person in that cell. The adjacent cell was stuffed full of black men who seemed to be without hope and perhaps ready to die. No explanation was offered. Days passed, Conrad received gruel and water for nourishment.

Finally, a man in a dirty uniform approach the cell and said, "Come with me."

Conrad's hands were tied, and he was placed into a horse-drawn buggy. He was taken to a place near the Harbor to stand in front of a man that the people called, "The Constable."

Conrad's situation was unusual so the questioning went on for some time. The Constable decided that Conrad should be turned over to the local military authorities for consideration and service in the Army of the Confederate States of America. His specific assignment while in service would be determined by the military authorities.

While waiting for his delivery to the military, he remained in the Charleston jail until he was eventually transported to a local military stockade. He was fourteen years old. Since he was never told the date of his birth or had a birthday celebration he did not know his actual age.

Several days later, three very young Confederate soldiers arrived to take him to the Charleston military headquarters. Since he was still a boy and had committed no civil crime, he was then taken to the Adjutant's office. From there he was assigned to a unit to begin his military training.

Conrad had never had a real bath in his life. His body order was strong from the confines of the ship. He was escorted to the Ashley River just adjacent to the military headquarters for a complete scrubbing. His hair was matted and hard. His body was covered with cracks that broke easily and bled profusely. Though water softened his hard and crusty skin. The salt water from the ocean had spilled back into the Ashley River at high tide irritating his whole body. The bathing process was eventually completed and a clean but ragged uniform was issued.

Conrad had never learned to count thus a marching cadence was difficult. He was issued a rifle, something he had never seen. It was explained to him that from this long piece of metal a projectile would exit at great speed. His job was to kill people to the front of where he would be standing. They were dressed in blue uniforms. On occasion, it would be needed for killing people who had dark skin.

For the first time in his young life, Conrad was a member of a group. The people around him seemed to accept him. They laughed at his accent and teased him about the sound of his voice. One day, a rather large group of young men who were training with Conrad were brought together to be sent by a train to the command of General Braxton Bragg, a 1837 graduate of the US military Academy. Conrad's group joined other young men from Tennessee, Mississippi and Louisiana to form a unit to serve near a small church in south-central Tennessee called Shiloh.

The train was to leave in the morning and arrive at another small town in northern Mississippi called Corinth. The trip would take three days. They would once again be formed into another unit of young soldiers to serve under the command of Captain Averial P. Jones. Once again Conrad heard the word "Yankee." It was his understanding from the Captain that a large number of Yankees were gathering some sixty miles north and were coming south to kill them.

Conrad was beginning to like his new friends and enjoy a full belly every day. He listened intently as the other young men laughed and joked about their superiority and the pending doom of the people in blue coming from the north.

On the morning of April 6, 1862, Conrad Teft heard the sounds of cannons, rifle fire and the inevitable screams. The news spread among the new recruits that their seasoned comrades were overrunning the northern lines commanded by Gen. William Tecumseh Sherman. This seemed to be a clear explanation for an expectation that it would be easy to shoot people wearing blue. After that day's victory, Conrad's reserve unit was directed to clean up the spoils of the battlefield that had been most recently won by the Confederate veteran forces. With confidence, Conrad moved with his reserve unit of one-hundred young soldiers to help with the wounded and take prisoners.

On the field, the work seemed easy enough, dead and dying bodies were everywhere. While picking up a canteen and rifle, Conrad heard an aggressive sound just behind him. As he turned he saw a person in a blue uniform charging with a shiny bayonet exposed and pointing toward him. Conrad was holding his knife and was about to cut belongings from the dead soldier near his knees. He swung the knife penetrating the attacking soldier's side leaving internal organs exposed. The young soldier in blue screamed and began to cry.

He sobbed saying, "I want my mother, you killed me."

He repeated these two phrases over many times. Sadness and disbelief overcame Conrad as he looked on. Another young Confederate soldier saw Conrad's dilemma and walked over exposing his rifle butt. He slammed it into the side of the young soldier's head. The sounds of despair and pleading stopped. Conrad remained on his knees and stared into the scene without moving. His mind swirled without explanation. He wanted to bend his head and cry.

The next morning, a group of raw recruits were now thrown into their own battle believing that they would carry the day and capture Pittsburgh's landing. They were unaware that General Grant had just received a large number of reinforcements commanded by General Buhl. They came in from Nashville, Tennessee during the night. The new veterans nearly doubled the number of soldiers wearing blue.

As Conrad and his confident buddies entered the second day of battle, the reality of the conflict had changed. They were quickly overwhelmed by the Union troops, so the Confederate soldiers began to run. In order to save themselves, they believed that they must get back to their lines at Corinth, their headquarters. This was a nine-mile run which few could sustain for any length of time. Many of the Confederate soldiers did not have boots or shoes so were running barefoot.

Nearly all of the young recruits were captured and brought behind the northern lines near Shiloh church. They were made to sit in large circles of about thirty soldiers. Conrad sat next to one of the soldiers from his unit. Both boys were exhausted and frightened. Guards were close at hand, so there was little hope for escape. Since they had to remain in the circle for an extended period of time, a hole was dug in the center of each circle for use as a latrine. An ordinary string was strung around the entire encampment at a height of about two feet. Within this encampment there were about ten circles. If any captured soldiers moved closer to the string than one foot, they would be shot immediately without question. The string became known as a "deadline" which is the origin of the word commonly used today.

Since there was no time for screening prisoners, Conrad and the other captives were loaded onto steamers heading for a prison camp outside of St. Louis, Missouri. The camp had few guards which resulted in very strict rules. Violations were met with immediate death. Prisoner exchanges were common during the early years of the Civil War. Thus, each prisoner was interviewed and made to sign a piece of paper promising not to return as a combatant in the Confederate Army. Conrad's interview took an unusual twist. At first, he refused to speak, but eventually he did describe his situation. His was a story that the capturing soldiers had never heard before. A Confederate soldier with a British accent who had never heard of the Civil War or slavery. He was set aside for further examination and placement. Conrad was strong and capable of physical work, so the Union Officer interviewing him felt he may be useful to them.

The officer who was to make the final decision regarding Conrad's disposition had been assigned to the third division of the 22nd infantry. This unit had been formed near the village of Ames, Iowa. Since many young soldiers were from central Iowa, there was a labor shortage in that area. Captain Anderson, the commander of these prisoners, was to deliver them to the St. Louis prison camp. Afterwards, he was to take a short leave to visit his family in central Iowa near Ames. Capt.

Anderson decided that he would not leave this unusual "British" prisoner in Missouri but, instead, would take Conrad to Central Iowa with him.

During his trip back home for his leave, Capt. Anderson decided that young Conrad should remain as a prisoner in central Iowa to help alleviate the labor shortage. It was evident that Conrad had no understanding of the conflict or even of the world he had been thrust into. Captain Anderson felt Conrad could help his father on the farm and would pose no threat to his mother, father or anyone else working on the farm.

Captain Anderson was a recent graduate of the West Point Military Academy. His home had always been in central Iowa. His appointment was made by Iowa's first senator, Sen. George W Jones. Captain Anderson's father, Jacob, was slightly connected to the state leadership because he was teaching and working with horticulture at the new land-grant college. Jacob's farm had been purchased by the US government for the purposes of teaching agriculture to Iowa citizens and other Americans because President Abraham Lincoln had decided that the first land-grant college should be located in Iowa near the town of Ames. Jacob now in his middle fifties had been employed by the college to do much of the teaching at this location.

Upon arriving at Captain Anderson's home, Conrad looked like a savior because everywhere people were looking for laborers. Jobs were everywhere, but workers were few. Most able-bodied young men had left to serve in the Civil War.

Since the Captain's furlough was for only seven days, a decision had to be made quickly regarding Conrad's future. All agreed that they would take a chance on him and that Captain Anderson would return to his unit and report what he had done. Conrad had no input into this final decision. He had no idea what was going to happen to him.

The first time in his life, Conrad began to believe that he might be in the care of people who were appeared to be concerned about others. He was given nourishing food and clean clothes. He slept on a soft bed, people smiled and seemed to show interest in his welfare. All of this was a brand-new experience. As he lay in his bed the first night, his mind wandered as he tried to imagine what was likely to happen in the upcoming days and weeks. With a smile on his face, he closed his eyes and fell into a restful sleep. There was something secure about this place. Morning came with a rap on the door. Breakfast was served and eaten. Work was about to begin.

The prior evening Jacob and Ardis, his wife, decided that a routine of farm chores would be assigned to Conrad. Since he was a prisoner, he would not be paid for his work. His compensation would consist only of board and room. His first responsibilities included the care and nurturing of a small group of animals. As he was able to demonstrate competence in these responsibilities, other duties would be assigned. Conrad began to show a deep concern for his work and a desire to please the adults around him.

This transition to a new life was simple for him but puzzling. He was leaving nothing behind so all of his efforts were aimed at trying to understand why this new world of caring people was offering such opportunities. A new ease in his smile began to appear. For the first time in his life, he felt actually happy as the nightmares of his past began to fade.

After the war ended, Conrad was recognized as a dedicated and hard worker so was paid a salary. He would work on this farm at Iowa State University for several decades before falling in love with a neighborhood girl. After Conrad and Sophie were married, they purchased and moved to a small farm near Jordan, Iowa.

CHAPTER 3

ADA

ON JUNE 12, 1894, a little baby girl was born to Conrad and Sophie Teft of Jordan, Iowa. Two neighbor ladies came from adjoining farms to help with the delivery. Conrad was very nervous, so the neighbor ladies had him hold the pan of water. This new baby was to be their second child and their first girl. They would name her Ada. Sophie had dreamed of a little girl to dress in pretty things and share her life in the kitchen. She also dreamed that this little girl in some way would favorably impact the lives of others.

Life was hard, but things were improving for people in rural America. Early on, Ada would embrace a love for little children. She had an older brother by four years named Raymond. He was kind and gentle and seldom brought frustration into her life. Ada loved and admired Raymond, and he was very protective and responsive to the needs of his little sister. The bond the brother and sister developed as very young children would stay intact until their deaths.

Ada always worked hard to please her parents and brother, Raymond. Roles were easily defined in this family. They were a family of loving, gentle people. Raymond helped his father work the farm fields while Ada performed chores in the house with her mother. They described themselves as a deeply Christian family that expected only harmony. The children attended a small rural school just outside of Jordan. The enrollment in the school was fifteen children. The days were idyllic as each child rejoiced at the success of each other and that of their friends.

Early in her school years, Ada began to help and teach girls and boys of all ages. Her teacher, Mrs. Morrison, seemed to understand that the bright and charming girl needed to be challenged with extra responsibilities. The school was only one room, so Ada became acquainted very early with the lessons for all eight grades. In the absence of Mrs. Morrison, Ada would help the students who were struggling with their lessons.

Most boys and nearly all the girls did not consider going on to secondary school which was usually located in the nearest town. A girl's job was in the home, and a boy's job was working the fields and tending the livestock. Ada, however, was different. At the age of twelve, she informed her mother and father that she would like to attend secondary school in Jordan. She loved to study and learn. She already knew at that young age that she wanted to attend the small land-grand college in the village of Ames only ten miles away. She kept that idea to herself because she knew that such an idea would be shocking to her parents. She needed time to get them slowly adjusted to the idea.

Over the years of secondary school, Ada dropped hints of college to her parents. She knew if she worked hard and received top grades in her studies, they would be more amenable to the idea. Ada studied hard and received high marks in all of her subjects. After such a successful experience in secondary school, she finally asked her parents if she could attend the small teacher's college in Ames. Because her studies in secondary school were so outstanding, they supported her desire to attend college.

Sophie always felt that Ada could accomplish something important, so she enthusiastically supported her daughter in her request to attend college. She was frequently teased and discouraged from achieving academic excellence while in secondary school, but she never wavered. She was a determined young lady with dreams of a brilliant future.

The family discussed and plotted over the summer how to handle the ten-mile distance to Ames. It was decided that Ada would live with an old lady, Jane, whom Sophie had become acquainted with through Jane's relatives. They attended the same church as the Teft family. Ada would return home every weekend to help the family with chores.

Jane was a jovial and kind lady who made the best potato pancakes that one could ever imagine. Ada grew fond of this breakfast, a breakfast that she would enjoy all of her life. The pancakes were hot and covered with a bit of butter. The maple syrup was warm. The room smelled with this delight every morning. Ada truly enjoyed her time with Jane. Their discussions were lively and thoughtful. Jane challenged Ada's thinking and encouraged her to look beyond their small corner of the world.

As expected, Ada performed in an exceptional manner. One day while sitting with her books and eating from her bag lunch, she saw a black man. She could not help but stare and wondered what life must be like when a person looked so different. He did not move and instead kept his books open in front of him while writing notes with his #2 soft lead pencil. Each day Ada returned to that spot to eat her lunch and study. Each day this man was also there. Same chair, same corner and same expression.

Finally, young Ada moved to the table where the black man sat. His face immediately changed to a broad smile as if to say, "You look great."

Ada returned the smile and said, "What are you studying?"

There was a long pause. Then slowly he remarked, "I am studying agriculture. What are you studying?"

Ada replied, "I am studying to be a teacher. I have wanted to teach little children all my life. Why would anyone want to study agriculture?"

His answer was long and confusing to Ada. She said, "What is your name?"

"My name is George Washington Carver."

Ada had no idea that she was visiting with a man who would become famous and a leader in the nation that she loved. George Washington Carver went on to be a botanist and a chemist while enrolled at Iowa State University. He did early research on crop rotations, peanut production and sweet potatoes. Mr. Carver was born a slave in Diamond Grove, Missouri, in the mid-1800s.

After nearly two years of study, Ada was given her license to teach in rural Midwestern schools. There was a shortage of teachers, so demand for her skills was high. However, school boards refused to hire a female who appeared to be so young. Ada's dreams seemed to be crushed as one rejection followed another.

Meanwhile, Ada's brother, Raymond, had fallen in love with Grace Weseman. Grace was the love of his life, and she lived in a very small village called Norcross in Minnesota. She was twenty-one years old and had lived her life in the shadow of her father, Simon. He maintained strict control over his daughters. They admired him and tried to obey his every word. He said he would grant Grace the permission to marry Raymond if she remained near the village of Norcross. Since Raymond desperately wanted to marry her, he asked his father to help him buy a farm near Elbow Lake, Minnesota, which was not far from Norcross. Conrad begged Raymond with promises of land to stay in central Iowa. However, Raymond was determined to marry Grace. After some consternation Conrad lent him the money to purchase a small farm near Elbow Lake.

Ada was excited to hear the news and believed that there would be schools in that area that would hire her to teach. She moved to Elbow Lake to live with Grace and Raymond. After several schoolboard interviews with skeptical old men, she was finally able to get a job offer. She was elated. She wondered, why did this school board in Elbow Lake agreed to hire her while others were so skeptical?

Although it was not apparent to her at the time, a well-connected young man named Paul Hartman sat on that school board. Paul, whose wife had died giving birth to their child who had also died, was the son of a very successful farmer and contractor. Ada was a beautiful young girl. She was tall and thin with long blonde locks framing her pretty face. Opportunities for courtship were everywhere, but Ada remained dedicated to her teaching career and did not pay much attention to the young men who tried to make her acquaintance.

Her brother, Raymond, protected her like a father for the first several years of teaching. Eventually Ada's heart was won by Paul Hartman.

School boards at that time usually required women who were married to resign their positions. However, with the help of Paul who still sat on the school board, the issue was not pressed. Ada was allowed to continue to teach the area children because everyone recognized what an outstanding teacher she had become.

Both she and Paul knew that she would be required to leave teaching should she become pregnant. Families in rural Minnesota did not want their children to see a woman who was soon to have a baby. They were afraid that this sight would induce children to ask, "How did that baby get in there?"

These things were not talked about. The policy was never considered a problem because it seemed to be well within the moral code of small communities and was never questioned. As Ada entered her sixth year of teaching, she became pregnant and would have her own baby in about six months.

She was so excited and knew that she would love this child more than life itself. She would resign the job that she enjoyed and wait for her baby to be born. She would miss teaching and seeing the children's excitement as they learned. But she was anxious to have her own child to love and to teach. Her commitment to this child would take her on a journey that would last for the rest of her life.

At long last she would now be able to kiss and cuddle her own little one. She and Paul decided to name their new baby boy, Lowell Wayne Hartman, a name that would become a legend in her small community. None of this would become apparent as she traditionally nurtured this infant forward.

Since her husband like his father was a large and successful farmer and an efficient road builder. She did not have to worry that adding this child to the family would be a financial burden. Ada happily spent the next months preparing their home for this child. Once Lowell was born, he behaved like Ada expected any infant to behave. He cried to be fed and changed. She cuddled and nurtured him. Paul began to speak of his dreams of having Lowell become a partner to help with this large farm and manage the successful contracting company when he grew up.

However, as the child neared six months of age, Ada began to notice that this little one did not respond to her cuddling with coos and smiles. He was not like the babies of her friends who seemed to respond warmly to their mothers. Ada's baby seemed to cry as he got older without an understandable provocation. He did not seem to react to his mother's nurturing with much interest. When calm, his affect was flat. When anxious, his responses seemed to be exaggerated. Like many young mothers, Ada tried to ignore these differences and imagined that they were the worries of an overprotective parent. She held her secrets in her heart. She did not discuss them with either her husband or her mother.

Ada refused to let herself worry and, instead, strongly denied to herself the behaviors Lowell was manifesting. During his developmental years, she affectionately began calling the baby "Wayne" which was his middle name. Her worries continued as he went from a baby to a toddler. Wayne, a toddler, did not show attachments or fears similar to other children.

As the toddler turned into a little boy, Paul asked, "Ada, do you see some unusual things about Wayne?"

Ada broke into a flood of tears. Her strong reaction to his question left Paul bewildered and shaken. She sobbed and wept, "Paul, I'm so scared."

The stage was set for endless conversations between the young couple. What was happening to their baby? What was wrong with him?

During the summer of Wayne's sixth year, his dog, Buddy, was run over by the heavy wheel of a construction scraper breaking the dog's pelvis and smashing its back legs. The dog, in great pain, lay dying in a small pathway near the farmyard. Wayne watched as part of this animal was crushed. The animal screamed much like a human. Ada stood nearby helplessly watching the animal's agony. She knew that her husband would have to kill the dog. As this was all happening, she noticed that six-year-old Wayne displayed a remarkable indifference to the animal.

He approached his crying mother and said, "I'm hungry, can I have some ice cream?" Ada had seen similar responses before but this one was much more graphic and much less understandable. She was stunned.

As Wayne grew older these incidences where he showed a remarkable lack of empathy grew more common. By now Ada and Paul had two other children with which to compare to Wayne. Their concern and puzzlement regarding Wayne's lack of empathy increased as their other children exhibited the emotional characteristics that their parents had expected to see in Wayne.

By now Wayne's unusual reaction to events which were either alarming or sad was very pronounced. He enjoyed playing with his younger siblings, but Ada, out of concern for them, refused to allow Wayne to be with them alone. She just did not trust him. He didn't seem to notice that his mother always remained nearby when the children were playing.

One summer day, Wayne was playing on a wooden farmyard fence. He slipped and drove a large sliver into the palm of his hand. Startled, he ran to his mother who recognized the large sliver and the associated pain. With long nails on her thumb and pointer finger, she tugged the sliver from the little boy's hand. She noticed that he did not seem to exhibit an emotional response to this injury. He did shed tears but not with the fear and anxiety that another child might express when confronted with the blood and pain of such an experience.

Ada felt as if she had no basis for understanding this phenomenon. Ada's love and affection and loyalty to Wayne prevented her from seeking help from her sister-in-law or her brother. This secret must be guarded and kept between her and Paul.

CHAPTER 4

TRAGEDY

Late on a summer afternoon in 1926, Ada began preparing a meal for the family. Food preparation with three children gave her little time for extra chores. Paul was in the cattle yard moving the herd and feeding them. He was so busy that he failed to notice it was time to come to the house for dinner. Wayne was in the yard stacking small logs; he was nine years old. Ada, somewhat harried, noticed that Wayne was available to fetch his father for the evening meal.

She said, "Wayne, go tell your father that dinner is ready."

The soon to be ten-year-old boy got up from the grass and began to move toward the cattle yard gate. Although he was usually obedient to his mother, he did respond more quickly than usual because this evening was special. Ada had prepared a pot roast with two apple pies, Wayne's favorite meal.

The barnyard gate had 2" x 10" boards crossing the opening held in place by four more 2" x 10" boards. The gate was heavy. A boy of Wayne's size had no chance of opening it. Instead he crawled upon the cross boards and looked for his father in the pasture.

His behavior was casual and unhurried since he had repeated this process many times. As he looked across the expanse of the pasture, he saw the cattle in a tight anxious group one-hundred yards away from the angry bull which shared the pasture with them.

Paul had told little Wayne many times to avoid the bull. Bulls were frequently unpredictable. The group of animals seemed to be cautious while staring at the bull as it drove its horns and hooves into something lying on the ground. The bull screamed in rage.

The object on the ground was his Dad who was not moving. Staring carefully with his heart pounding, Wayne clearly recognized the pieces of colored clothing that Paul was wearing as he left for the barnyard that day. His eyes grew wide as the bull screamed. Minutes seemed to have turned into an eternity. Wayne's mind raced and became dull as he continued to stare at the calamity that had befallen his father.

Emotional responses were always hard for Wayne but he did manage to collect his thoughts. He raced to his mother. He was trying to understand what had just happened. He feared he already knew. As Wayne breathlessly verbalized bits and pieces of the happening in the cattle yard, Ada screamed to no one in particular and raced from the house to the pasture.

The bull continued to ravage her husband's dead body as she watched. Her first thought was to pull his lifeless body from the scene. She somehow wanted to stop this out-of-control tragedy, yet she knew she could not stop the angry bull by herself.

She thought, "I cannot drive the bull from my husband's body. I must tend to the small children in the house and not frighten them with my tears."

There was no way to call for help. There were no adults nearby. Never having prepared herself for such a happening, she demanded of herself that she think quickly for a workable solution. There was no phone and the nearest neighbor lived nearly one mile away.

Her mind raced as she thought, "How do I get someone's attention?" Nothing was evident.

Many times, Paul had suggested that she learn to drive. Other women in the area were starting to consider this new freedom.

Ada continually said, "No, I only want to be a wife and mother, and you can drive to get whatever we need."

Beside the barn sat a 1921 Model A Ford. She had watched John operate it many times but paid little attention. On one occasion he had asked her to help get the car started, so she did after he explained the necessary steps in the process. A single training event was not much, but that was all she had.

She quickly loaded the anxious and tearful children into the car. They were too young to be left alone.

She had seen Paul work the levers but had never paid much attention. Through the screams and tears and cries of the children, she lowered herself into the front seat by the steering wheel. The engine obediently started. She attempted to push the lever that she had seen make the car go. She did not notice that Paul had pushed the clutch and then pushed on the big lever.

She smashed the car into gear. Mechanical parts banged in pain as the car began an ugly jerk forward. She had not noticed that there was another pedal that made the car move. She would have to settle for the slow jerking one-mile journey to the Johnson's. The little ones were crying. Martha sobbed with silent gasps. Wayne sat in the seat next to her without affect, staring straight over the front hood of the car.

This was uncharted territory. The travel lasted about ten minutes with Ada arriving near the Johnson house. She smashed the car into a gate and fence in an effort to stop it. The calamity in the yard was immediately noticed by the Johnson children. They came running with anxious uncertainty.

Although they recognized Ada, they were unsure as to what to make of her approach. They had never seen her driving the car. She was behaving in a way that they had never seen before. Her two little ones were in the rear part of the car crying hysterically and attempting to get to their mother's side.

The situation was further complicated by the fact that the Johnsons and the Hartmans were not very friendly neighbors. Mr. Johnson was a severe alcoholic and always felt that the Hartmans acted like they were of higher status and looked down upon his family. The Johnsons fourteen children all seemed to be standing around the smashed car. The Hartman children piled out of the car to join the Johnson children. Between seventeen upset children running about and herself, the Johnson yard looked like an anthill with ants busily storing food for the coming winter.

Ada screamed for Mrs. Johnson, a tired looking woman who appeared years past her thirty-ninth birthday. Olivia Johnson came running from the house with a dish rag and rubbing her hands. Without saying anything, the two women realized that they had to work together to solve a problem that neither completely understood. Mrs. Johnson was able to make no sense of the loud multiple conversations occurring all at once.

She reached for Ada's terror filled face, grabbed her shoulders and said, "What is happening to my lovely neighbor. Please tell me?"

Out of sympathy, Olivia began to cry without knowing why Ada was hysterical. Ada began to tell the story of the bull and her husband. Olivia immediately knew that this was a horrible tragedy. Many times, she had been told by her husband and her father that bulls were always dangerous.

She hollered for her fourteen year old daughter, Elizabeth, "Get your father, we need his help immediately."

Olivia believed that Elizabeth was her most competent child. While everyone was either crying or confused by the crying, Elizabeth ran to the house for her shoes. She usually spent her summers in bare feet, but running amongst the hard ground and stubbles to reach her father required shoes. She laced them tightly and ran toward the field to find her father who was making corn bundles.

Tom was pulling a corn binder with two draft horses through the tall standing corn. He had to stop the binder every eight feet to wrap twine around the collected corn stocks. The horses snorted while the corn binder made dozens of loud, odd sounds. It was difficult to get her father's attention. Elizabeth had to get dangerously close to the moving machine in order to command his attention. She had run nearly one-half mile before finding Tom and the horses. When she grabbed the lead draft horse's bit, the animal stopped immediately. Tom stared at his daughter with a look of confusion and annoyance on his face

He got down from the binder seat and reached for his daughter. She was now talking through hysterical tears.

Elizabeth screamed, "Mr. Hartman is dead. He has been killed by the bull."

Tom understood immediately. He said, "Elizabeth lead the horses back to the barn and have your brother help you release the harnesses."

Getting back to the house was difficult for Tom. He was a heavy smoker (rolled his own) and almost always drank himself to sleep. Gasping for air, he ran for the house tripping over the corn stubble and pulling himself up multiple times.

Arriving at the house, he looked at the disheveled Ada and said, "What happened to Paul and where is he?"

Through tears, Ada answered, "He has been trampled by the

bull and is in the cattle yard. He is most certainly dead. Please help us to get him out."

Without thinking, Tom ran to his old car, started the engine and drove at full speed to the cattle lot where he expected to find Paul and the bull. He had never driven the car that fast before. He was surprised. The car bounced along the rutted road. Tom hit his head on the ceiling of the auto several times. The roof of the car had no padding, so each bump was painful. The last big jolt left Tom a bit dizzy as he stopped the car near the wooden gate.

He cautiously left the vehicle because he dreaded the scene he was about to view. He had seen people die in the prime of their lives before because he was a veteran doughboy in World War I. Such scenes were always traumatic.

Sure enough, the bull stood with a raging anger but was no longer striking at the body with its feet. Tom's face was sober as he looked at the unbelievable scene before him. He was helpless to do anything to help Paul. A tear of sadness fell on his cheek.

He knew that he could not get the bull away from Paul's body. He could not safely enter the pasture to retrieve the body. He puzzled over what action to take. After a few anxious minutes, he remembered he had kept his old M1 rifle from World War I. Slowly he returned to the car. It was still running because in his haste to get to the pen, he had forgotten to shut it off. He got into the car and began the one-mile trek back for the gun.

When he reached the house, he climbed the steps and went to the bedroom that he and Olivia shared. The weapon stood in the back of the closet still in its case. High on the shelf in the closet above the clothes were ten bullets that he had hidden in his footlocker for shipment back to Elbow Lake. He

Tragedy

never imagined that he would ever use this weapon again, but that would now change.

He took the clip from the bolt action rifle and inserted five shells. It seemed that he had done this type of loading of the rifle just yesterday. His skills had not diminished after eight years. The two families stood in awe near the Johnson house as Tom laid the rifle on the back seat of the old car. As he started to leave, he told Ada that he would go to her brother, Raymond, and ask for help. Slowly traveling the one-mile back to the Hartman farm, he drove the car near to the pasture fence. He slowly opened the door and reached around to pick up the weapon of death. He pulled back the bolt allowing the deadly shell to enter the firing chamber. That clicking sound brought back tearful memories of 1917 and 1918 when he had taken the life from two young German soldiers.

The bull cast a menacing stare toward Tom without realizing that its life would be over in a matter of seconds. Tom rested the rifle on the wooden fence. He had done this before in the war. He pointed the gun midway up the bull's body and just behind the front shoulder. There lay the animal's rapidly beating heart. Tom pulled the trigger. The gun responded with authority. Already facing Tom, the bull was beginning to prepare to attack another intruder. The impact of the bullet jarred the large animal's body. A tiny hole was visible, blood was beginning to emerge. Still facing Tom, the animal's face went from rage to apparent puzzlement.

The beast stood for nearly ten seconds and then slowly bent its front legs to its knees as if getting ready to pray. The motions were slow as the large body slowly rolled to its side. The animal took a deep gurgling breath and lay limp.

The beast lay twenty feet from Tom, just to the side of Paul's mangled body. Even though Tom had seen many mutilated bodies in France, he lacked the courage or perhaps stomach to crawl over the fence and remove Paul's body parts from the cattle yard.

With the smell of gunpowder in his nostrils, Tom slowly backed away from the fence and walked toward his old car with the motor still running. He drove the two miles to Ada's brother's house where Raymond was cleaning equipment that he had been using for milking cows.

He looked up and saw Tom approaching. This was unusual because Tom had never been to Raymond's farm before. Raymond was puzzled as Tom approached the barn. Raymond, a kind person, warmly greeted Tom as though they were good friends. Tom offered no response.

He faced Raymond and said, "Raymond, your sister's husband has been killed by their bull. I shot the bull but could not bring myself to touch Paul's body. You should go to your sister who is at my house. I will go to the town and inform the sheriff."

The two men shared a warm and sad embrace.

"After I talk to the sheriff, I will return to your sister's home and guard the remains," tearfully Tom responded.

Tears tumbled down Raymond's face. He was a soft and gentle man who showed respect for nearly everyone. His sadness was further exacerbated by the fact that he had loaned the bull to Paul for the purposes of breeding cattle in his herd. Raymond's heartbreak was extreme as he collected himself to join his sister at Tom's house.

By mid-afternoon, men from town arrived to remove Paul's body from the cattle yard. The mortician from Elbow Lake handled the body parts as gently as possible and placed them in a large black bag. The hearse stood waiting nearby as the mortician returned to it with Paul's remains.

Ada wanted desperately to go back to their farmyard to observe the happenings, but Raymond would not allow her to return. He stood firmly by her side as she continued to vent her grief. Olivia remained close by to help lend support to Ada and to watch the children who milled about not sure what was going on. Although Wayne knew what had happened, he remained indifferent to his mother's grief. Instead, he tried to entice the younger children into playing games as they waited to learn what was happening. There was muted play among them as they questioned Wayne about their mother's grief. He continued to shrug his shoulders and voice that he knew nothing. Olivia had told the older children to say nothing to the younger ones because she felt it should be Ada who explained to them what had happened to their father.

The small children ran about and complained to Olivia and Ada who were now sitting in rockers on the Johnson's old unpainted porch. Olivia shielded Ada from responding to the questions and problems as the small children looked for answers. She tried to solve every issue they presented. Ada sat in silence. Her small children played freely with the Johnson children who also were too young to realize what had happened. The older Johnson children formed a little group away from the little ones as they tried to make sense of what had happened and what impact it would have on the Hartman family.

Olivia, an emotional woman, attempted to relieve Ada's anguish. In an attempt to comfort, she placed her arm over Ada's shoulder. This was difficult for her since Ada had vastly more social status than she. She worried that Ada may reject her offer of comfort but none came forth. Olivia did know that times like these changed long-held beliefs by people, but she wasn't sure that Ada would accept such a gesture that seemed to cross social norms. Olivia felt a kinship with Ada and just knew that she would remain a faithful and loving friend to this heart-broken woman for all time. Although Ada had hardly spoken to Olivia before today, she willingly accepted her caring gesture. She, too, would deeply love and respect Olivia throughout her life.

The memory of these moments was burned into Ada's being. Occasionally she lifted her head trying to make sure that her children were behaving in a manner that was acceptable. Each time she looked around, her eyes briefly stopped and observed her son, Wayne. As she expected, he appeared remarkably detached and unaffected. Today, like never before, she knew that her son had a unique understanding of the world, something very different from her own. She had already worried for thousands of hours that she would be unable to change the dark side of this growing boy. From the day of his birth, she had loved him and continued to love him more than life itself.

The loss of Paul seemed heavier than anything she could bear. Paul had fulfilled every dream a woman could have as she built her family. He had helped her cope with her growing concerns about Wayne. He had shown patience when working with Wayne and had remained constantly optimistic as Wayne seemed to grow more detached

CHAPTER 5

RAYMOND'S SUPPORT

Ada knew now that the emotional support that Paul had provided would have to be supplied by her loving brother, Raymond. Raymond and his new wife, Grace, had a four-month-old little girl named Rosetta. Raymond knew that they lived too far away to provide Ada with the support she would need to manage the farm. He talked with Grace and she agreed that they would need to live closer in order to help Ada with the farm. They decided to move their small family to the smaller home on Ada's farm while Ada would remain in the home she had occupied with Paul.

Ray had frequently heard Ada speak of her worries regarding her son. While trying to take care of the two families and the two farms, Raymond became more acutely aware of his nephew's dysfunction. As he grew older, Wayne had become more difficult for Ada to manage. Raymond decided that he would take on the task of helping Ada raise Wayne by bringing him into his own home. He had also learned by this time that this boy's view of the world and his relationship to it were very different from his own. Although he frequently felt frustration and anger, he never allowed himself to show either emotion toward Wayne.

The boy was detached but not angry. Wayne had little success with the projects that were assigned to him by his uncle.

Raymond did not see the boy as particularly dim witted even as he seemed to have difficulty grasping the simplest concepts. Raymond, instead, felt the boy lived in a world that he did not understand. At times, he felt fear for himself as he tried to explain tasks. Grace did not approve of Wayne being in their home because she worried that something might happen to her little girl when she was unable to stay close to her. She refused to let Rosetta be alone with Wayne because he seemed so unpredictable and detached. For these reasons, she also felt worried and anxious around Wayne.

Ada continued to live in the home she had occupied with Paul. She adjusted to the new circumstances surrounding her family. Raymond operated both farms. Since Paul frequently hired workers for the various tasks, Raymond continued this practice for his sister's farm and his own.

As the years went by, Raymond noticed that his interests were moving away from farming and toward business. He really enjoyed managing both farms and dealing with the issues that arose throughout the year, but he dreamed of other challenges. He had become particularly interested in the new and colorful automobiles that were being manufactured and sold throughout the country.

For the first time, Wayne showed an interest in something. He shared his uncle's enthusiasm for cars. He could not take his eyes off them and would make every effort to sit in them while pretending to drive. Raymond also had developed a passion for automobiles and hoped that one day he would be able to give up farming and start a successful automobile dealership.

As Raymond's interest in cars and owning a car dealership grew, so did young Wayne's interest. He now tried to spend a lot of time with his uncle Ray looking at and driving

Raymond's car. In 1927, there were few restrictions on driving cars. Wayne frequently frightened everyone by getting into the car and traveling to Raymond's nearby farm without any adult assistance. He was only twelve.

Although this unassisted driving was a problem, both Ray and Ada agreed that Wayne's car interest might be a way to shape this unresponsive boy to a future that could be productive.

By the time Wayne was fourteen, Ray began to trade in cars from his farm. Wayne loved working and playing at his uncle's small selection cars that he had for sale. He was frequently truant from school but since he seemed to be doing something, his uncle and his mother placed few restrictions on him.

CHAPTER 6

THE FAMILY NEXT DOOR

THE ZIMMER FAMILY LIVED NEXT DOOR to the Tefts on the outskirts of Elbow Lake. The two homes were separated by a six-hundred-foot deep grove of trees. During the summer months, when the windows were open, screams and shouts could be heard almost daily emanating from the Zimmer house. Ray and Grace were tightlipped and did not reveal any of their worries as to what might be going on in the Zimmer home. Folks in Elbow Lake minded their own business.

The Zimmer household consisted of a mother, Rose, a father named Edward and a little boy named Sam. Rose was kind and gentle. She often visited Gace but never revealed what caused the commotion that could be heard as far away as the Teft house. Grace did not ask even though Rose often appeared with visible bruises. Grace guessed they were caused by Edward who was unfriendly and curt when spoken to by the Tefts. Grace and Raymond often discussed the neighbors and felt that Edward was mean and often violent toward his family. However, they remained silent toward the neighbors adhering to the code of "mind your own business."

Sam was an optimistic boy who believed that if he tried hard enough he could win the approval of his vicious father. He tried hard to do the tasks that his father ordered. Ray remembered one time when Sam was eight years of age, he was trying to help his father move a two thousand pound bull from a small pen in the barn. His efforts were unsuccessful and led to his father's rage. To Raymond's horror, Edward lifted the little boy from the pen by his hair and threw him into the warm, soft pile of animal waste. Edward in a rage held him under the soft manure until Raymond grabbed his shirt and pulled him off Sam.

Edward screamed at the child, "You are no good, you will never amount to anything."

Edward left the barn while Raymond attended to the boy. The child gasped for air and eventually gained enough strength to stand with Ray's help. The cries from the child took the form of deep gasps in quick succession with deep breaths. Sam was covered with animal waste in his nose, his eyes and his ears. Ray took Sam to his house through the trees. As they approached the house, they saw Grace standing in the doorway with little Wayne. Wayne studied his little friend curiously unable to understand what might have happened.

Grace asked, "Sam, what happened to you?"

Through tears and sobs Sam answered, "I was bad, my dad says I am no good, he tries hard to help me be a good boy."

Raymond did not contradict the boy but shook his head back and forth letting Grace know there was much more to the story than Sam had sobbed. Grace stood in stunned silence as she reached out to Sam. Wayne remained at a curious distance and did not show any emotion to the scene that was unfolding before him. When Grace decided to go to the Zimmers to get clean clothes for Sam, Wayne drifted off into the backyard to play with his toys leaving Ray and Sam to stand together in the front room.

Edward was still fuming when Grace arrived for the clothes. Rose handed them to her and suggested that Sam stay with them that night. She was worried that his return might further enrage Edward.

Sam liked the idea of staying overnight with the Tefts because he could play with Wayne. He was seldom allowed to play with other children because his father demanded that he help with the multiple tasks on their small acreage on the edge of town.

Sam was often hit and humiliated as his father tried to make him a good boy. Sometimes in the morning before school, Edward would holler at Rose over some small indiscretion whipping the little kitchen into a frenzy. As his rage built, he would turn his focus and resulting aggression toward the little boy. Most often he would drive his fingernail along the side of Sam's face, eventually striking his eye causing bleeding and swelling.

Sam hated to go to school with these marks and would make up stories about what had happened to him. He was afraid that everyone would know that he had been bad. He felt ashamed. He did not want to be a bad boy. He knew that saying anything to others about his father's violence would be breaking the fourth commandment, "Honor thy father and thy mother." This probably would mean that he would have to go to hell if the world ended that day. Sam worried about this a lot because the end of the world was frequently a topic of conversation in the Zimmer house.

One thing that remained consistent throughout the turmoil was his new friend, Wayne, who made no judgment of him and would listen to his worries without response. Other children at school often make fun of Sam and criticized his family, but Wayne never joined the others in their taunting. Sam tried to fight back because he never once considered that his family did not deserve such a warm loving child. He just knew that his parents were right. They praised other children in his presence. While at the same time talking to others about Sam's many failures. He did not understand how other children could be so good and praiseworthy, and he was so bad despite trying so hard to be good.

Edward frequently reminded Sam that he did not deserve the loving and caring father that he had. He frequently said, "You owe me. I gave you life."

One evening the Zimmers drove to Jacob Meyer's house. Sam was excited because the Meyers had three older boys ranging in age from ten to fourteen. For a while the three older boys played in the house with eight-year-old Sam but they grew bored and drifted outside. Once outside, the older boys decided a prank was in order, so they grabbed Sam and tied him to a tree in the grove behind their house. Then they laughed and teased Sam before going back to the house leaving him tied to the tree. At first Sam acted childlike, he expressed anger and frustration as he tried to loosen the ropes, but as darkness began to set in, he began to feel terror. He screamed and cried for help. No one came.

Later as the Zimmer family prepared to return to their home, Rose said, "Where is Sam, he hasn't been here all evening?"

Not revealing the truth, the three boys said, "We think we know where we can find him."

Instead of going directly to the spot where Sam was tied, they made frightening noises and pretended like there were people in the woods whose intent was to hurt Sam. They created more panic in the little boy before coming to the tree where Sam was tied and removing the bindings.

As they all made their way back to the house, Sam was crying with gasps and tears. What Sam expected to be a night of fun and play with the big boys turned into a night of terror that would lead to many more nights filled with terror and horrible nightmares.

As Sam came into the house, Edward said, "Grow up, don't be a baby."

Life in Sam's family did not change much over the next

several years. Sam was now fourteen and Wayne had just turned sixteen. Wayne informed Sam that he was taking a farm job, ten miles away. He was about to leave Sam without a friend. Until this time, Sam never considered how much he cared for this boy who said nothing.

Wayne felt no remorse about his departure. He never really attached to anyone. All that Sam knew was that Wayne never had a bad word to say to him. Somehow saying nothing was comforting to Sam.

Days before Wayne was going to leave on his new adventure, he and Sam visited. Wayne knew of the abuse that Sam had endured. Wayne knew that the violence in Sam's home became more frequent and more violent as Sam grew older.

Sam asked through tears, "What am I going to do without you?"

Wayne held his head low and said, "If he were my father, I would kill him" as he left for a seat in his uncle's car giving no more thought to what he had just said to Sam.

Days passed and turned into weeks. Without his usual friend, Wayne, the tension continued to grow for Sam. Mid-morning on a warm summer day, Sam's hurt exploded into rage. He had completed his usual farm chores and set about to enter the farm house and have some warm bread with fresh peanut butter. Almost immediately, Edward burst into the house screaming about how the neighbor lady was going to town and it was only Wednesday. How could someone be so arrogant and irresponsible as to need to make a six-mile trip so soon after she had just been there two days ago.

Edward's rage quickly built into another wild episode. He screamed at his wife and then turned toward Sam. His eyes were flashing with hate. Sam knew that he was in the crosshairs of another attack. Once again, he was filled with fear and terror.

Edward grabbed Sam by the shoulders and threw him against the wall. The wall had a protruding board for hanging pots and pans. Sam's head hit the board, drawing blood. Again, he was grabbed and thrown to the floor. Edward delivered two blunt kicks from his hard boots that he wore in the barn. Sam screamed and cried.

When his dad turned away, Sam quickly bound to his feet and ran toward the back door. As he passed the gun cabinet, he grabbed his father's rifle and ran to the barn. He lay on the floor of the barn with his rifle pointing toward the open barn door. He knew that his father's rage would not easily subside.

Sam was very good with a rifle and could hit a moving rabbit at twenty-five yards. As he lay in the animal waste waiting for his father to continue the attack, his heart was pounding, tears running down his face as he reminded himself of Wayne's advice.

In what seemed like hours, Edward finally entered the barn and faced the rifle. His cursing accelerated into screams of rage at Sam.

Edward screamed, "You are no good and never will be any good."

Edward began to move down the fifteen-foot path toward the rifle as he raged at Sam. Sam knew he could easily kill him, but should he? He thought about what Wayne would do.

Aiming just above Edward's right knee, Sam pulled the trigger. His life had now changed forever. Edward fell to the barn floor cursing and swearing and threatening Sam. Crying, Sam stood up and walked toward his father with the look of hatred and pity. Sam slowly walked from the barn and continued walking toward Ray and Grace's house. He had left forever.

PART TWO

THE SCHREADER FAMILY

CHAPTER 7

GERMAN BEGINNINGS

THE YEAR 1895 MARKED THE INVENTION of the first internal combustion bus that drove from Sieon, Germany, to Munich. Martin Schreader was eighteen years old. He was a hard-working young man who had many dreams of a fulfilling future. Opportunities were few, but he did not discourage easily. His family was very poor so they could offer little help. Martin was growing up near a young girl named Martha who was always his best friend and playmate. He was now beginning to notice her as something more than just a friend next door. She was developing into a beautiful young woman. As youngsters they spent many hours playing children's games, laughing, and sharing their dreams and their worries. As their youth passed, their appreciation for each other as a friend turned into a mutual love.

They lived in a small village by the name of Simonwaldt which was just seven kilometers East of a much larger community called Freiburg. These places were located in the Black Forest of the German Republic. Martin and Martha rarely left this small community. Martin only traveled three times to Freiburg during his eighteen years. Martha had never visited the city. Work consisted of tending to a farmer's three milk cows, twenty pigs and birds of various types. His days were filled with backbreaking labor, yet his wages were small. Martha spent her years helping her mother, washing clothes for her father and seven siblings. She worked at a small bakery near her home for very little money. Because time alone was minimal, privacy had become important to these two young adults. As their relationship grew more intimate, a child began to grow in Martha's body. Together they were about to face a life crisis that would include the religious criticism of their parents and the German government. Together they managed the crisis which infused their lives with a combativeness and trust that would last for all of their days.

In the late 1800s, the Bismarck took control of the country and made it a German Republic with himself as the head of government. The two primary religious organizations Lutherans and Catholics heavily influenced the country's new laws. One of the new laws decreed that marriage was a privilege, so a large fee was placed on anyone wishing to obtain a license to marry. The idea was that if poor people had children, the country would not be able to take care of its citizens. Martin and Martha had no money, so they faced the possibility that they could never marry. Any hope of getting out of poverty was dashed by another law that required large deposits before land could be purchased. Martin's livelihood would have to come from the land. It was unlikely that Martin and Martha would be able to find enough money to purchase a license for marriage let alone be able to make a down payment on some land. Their disappointed parents could offer no financial support so purchasing land was also out of the question.

When Martin told the local priest about their situation, he told him that the church had a small amount of money that would be able to cover their passage to America. Communities and churches were able to maintain small endowments to help pay for passages to America after these repressive laws were passed. This helped the Country to rid itself of poor people who would never be able to contribute to the wealth of the German Republic.

Another repressive law also enabled the authorities to remove infants from their mothers should the church and community decide that they were incapable of providing adequately for the little ones. Usually, the children were placed with government workers or military families. Martha refused to consider this dreadful possibility for her child. She would take her chances in America.

CHAPTER 8

THOUGHTS ABOUT LEAVING GERMANY

THE ONLY UNDERSTANDING of what they might be facing by traveling to a new country came from a few letters that former villagers sent to their German relatives after settling in America. Most letters were encouraging. However, there were no letters from families who had met with difficulties or even disasters. Martha and Martin had only read stories of success, so their optimism was high. Small amounts of free land in the American West were still available for settling. They decided to try to make their way to a place called Mobridge, South Dakota, their new home. All indications were that this would be a good place to begin a new family. Weeks of anxious conversation followed. Doubts had to be thought through and plans clarified.

Word quickly spread that Martin and Martha were about to do the unthinkable by traveling together without wedding vows. Such a circumstance caused much discussion among folks in town. Most were shocked at the prospect but seemed to understand the limitations of the young people's situation.

During the days when gossip was running rampant throughout the town, a lady with four children, Etta Sathoff, approached Martha in the bakery while she was working. Etta's husband had recently been killed while cutting lumber in the woods nearby. Etta had already received assurances from the little village that she would receive money for passage to America. She was told that if she did not accept this offer, her children might be taken from her. Those threats were terrifying. She told Martha that she had a cousin in Parkersburg, Iowa. Her cousin offered to help once she arrived in America. Without expecting much hope for a new life for herself, she knew that she would be able to create new opportunities for her children's future success.

Etta offered to help the young couple with their plan. She also told them that there was free land available in America which confirmed to the young people what they had already heard. She told of green fields, where crops grew tall and food was plentiful. She told of how people in Iowa who did not want to farm could get good paying jobs at the John Deere plow and tractor company in a village called Waterloo. She also believed that getting married in America would not be a problem.

The young couple and Mrs. Sathoff quickly became close friends. They started planning together in earnest, but anxiety always loomed above the three of them. Although they were reassured that passage money would be made available, they worried about the trek to the ocean and the Atlantic crossing. Since they didn't speak English, they worried about talking to people once they arrived in America. How would they find a place to stay? Where would they get food? How would they find transportation West?

Martin made a contact with his cousin, Jacob, in Freiburg. He asked for help to make the four-hundred-kilometer trek to the port of Hamburg to board a ship heading for America. Jacob was an accomplished clockmaker. He made specialty clocks (cuckoo clocks) to be sold in America to wealthy people. Each year he loaded his wagons for the long trek to the port. He had been doing this for nearly fifteen years, and, as a result, he was acquainted with shipping companies and their practices. He was considered by all to be a smart and honorable craftsman and a reliable man for consultation.

The government and the elders of the village encouraged a quick departure. Martha packed up all of their belongings in a small box. She had to leave many treasures behind. As the departure date grew closer, Martha would hear her mother privately weeping in her bed each morning. She knew that she would never see her loving Martha again.

A small wagon arrived from Simonwaldt one morning. The seven people readied themselves for the one-hour ride to Freiburg. A few members from their small church arrived and said prayers for their safe travel. Hugs and best wishes marked the gathering. The draft horses responded to the aggressive voice of the wagon driver. The small wagon loaded with anxious souls disappeared into the morning darkness. They would never return. By now Martin and Martha had shed all of their weaknesses and replaced them with a strong determination and quiet confidence.

The wagon bumped and jerked forward to the clickety-clacks of the horse's feet and the crunching of the narrow, tall wheels against the hard-packed dirt road. Looking up, the stars seemed to be busy forming a map above the trees to encourage the new travelers. As the small group moved slowly down the winding trail, they pointed out houses with thatched roofs releasing spirals of smoke from their chimneys. Breakfast was beginning for the hungry occupants. The sky began to show tiny blades of light above the hills as the travelers moved through villages. Streets were empty, dogs barked and occasionally a curtain opened to gaze at the people in the wagon as they passed. Their first stop would be in the city of Frieburg just ahead.

The wagon moved toward the center of the city to find cousin Jacob. His shop was located near the town square. There stood a large wagon fully loaded with clocks. Four draft horses were hitched to it prepared for the twelve days of travel. There was scant room for the travelers among the large wooden boxes. Jacob was uncertain about this idea of including the extra people since he had never loaded his wagon so heavily. Would the wagon support all this extra weight? Would the horses be able to pull this heavy load for twelve days?

CHAPTER 9

THE JOURNEY ACROSS A NATION

WITH CONSIDERABLE APPREHENSION AND AMBIVALENCE, Jacob decided that another wagon would be necessary for this heavy load. Martin would have to drive another set of horses. His travelers had no money to offset the cost of the second wagon and only had money for small amounts of food. Jacob knew that he would have to bear the expense of the second wagon and hoped that someday his travelers would have enough money to repay him for his consideration. He had managed to gather a small savings from years of carving and adjusting clocks, so he would use that to cover the additional expense. As a morally righteous man, he felt that he had no choice but to go ahead with this journey despite the extra expense. Etta and her three children would ride in the wagon with Jacob while Martin and Martha would ride in the second wagon.

Martha sat beside Martin claiming the only cushion that would reduce the jarring force from the steel springs holding the seat. They both worried that the twelve days of bumping might result in the loss of their baby. They prayed and held each other tightly as the drama began. The morning air was cool, as the sleeping city of Freiburg disappeared forever.

The rattling wagons creaked and cringed along the harshly, rutted dirt road in the Black Forest. The road was without mercy as the wagons lurched from side to side. Trees hung over the narrow roads and occasionally slapped against the tender skin of the wagon's occupants leaving red marks on faces and arms as they shoved the branches aside. They saw small homes with thatched roofs spread along the route. Children were helping their mothers work in the gardens by their houses. It was sad for Martin, Martha and Etta to gaze on these sights knowing they would never see them again.

Jacob watched over the young couple in the second wagon as they bumped along on their journey. He worried continually that one of the wagons would break down and require expensive work. He had used most of his savings to secure the second wagon so would have no money for any repairs.

Jacob drove the first wagon with a loaded shotgun on his lap. There were still marauders and thieves hiding in the remote landscape of this newly formed country. As they moved along, the trees of the Black Forest disappeared and began to turn into a rolling landscape where there were fewer trees. As the trees diminished, the wealth of the people decreased. Although it was a time of peace in Germany, it was also a time of poverty. Hardship was everywhere in the rolling hills. Whenever the party had to stop, there were always local people begging for food for their children.

These sad sights increased Martha and Martin's determination to leave for America as they held each other closely on the high wagon seat. Although they had no idea as to what hardships their future may bring, their determination grew with each kilometer of the journey. The first phase of the journey took them to a city called Stuttgard where they saw a large roughly, constructed building where people were engaged in making shiny buggies and a primitive thing that would day be called a horseless carriage. Slowly passing by they read the name on the side of the building - Mercedes-Benz.

As the wagons moved north they passed through another city called Heidelberg. There they saw a school of higher learning. The school sign read that people at the school were debating such things as philosophy, religion and mathematics. Martha and Martin wondered how these people could live without working. The trail came close to the larger city of Frankfurt just adjacent to a village called Selginstadt. There they secured a barge to cross the river Main. A small river but deep enough to allow for barge traffic. The river barge operator was a man by the name of Adam Zoller. Martin told Adam that they were headed for America.

Adam said, "My son, Peter, also has gone to America. He bought a prosperous farm in a place called Sheldon, Iowa. He is very happy in America. I hope you will find happiness there too."

Adam was proud of his son and tried to offer as much advice and comfort as he could to these travelers. Martha, Martin and Etta had many questions and he assured them that the trip would bring them prosperity and fulfillment.

The next six days of the trip would take them to the port city of Hamburg. The wagon continued to be uncomfortable constantly jarring their young bodies. Luckily, the jarring did not disrupt Martha's pregnancy. It seemed as if the fetus would also hang on to the promise of a new life in America. Hamburg filled the hearts and minds of the young couple with excitement and anticipation with a tinge of terror. This would be their last stop in the Motherland to which they would never return.

Hamburg was a city filled with energy and activity. People were busy selling, planning, and preaching about all sorts of things from potions to religion. Fortunes were being made. Dreams were being crushed. To the new travelers not much of this made sense. Jacob made his way through the maze of excitement to the docks where passenger ships and cargo ships were being loaded. The age of the sailing vessel was in the past. The harbor was filled with side wheelers marked by black smoke from the soft coal burning in their bellies. Coal dust made everything near the docks dirty and sticky.

Jacob and Martin maneuvered the wagons through the crowds near the docks. Jacob was able to find a man whom he recognized who might be able to help navigate the masses of tangled people.

"Where is the ship, the *California*, and when does it depart?" He asked.

"Where can we find a room?" asked Martin. The answers were quick in coming,

"The *California* is five ships ahead, and it departs in three days for New York," replied the dock master. "There are rooms all along the harbor, but most are not cleaned and have problems with rats."

Martin cringed at the prospect of dirty rooms with rats, but he did not know what else to do because Martha needed to be able to lie down and rest before going out to sea. Etta was also tired and her children were exhausted from the long, arduous trip.

The small group decided that they must endure the prospect of filthy rooms and rats to stay close to the *California* as it was readying itself to set out to sea. A man grabbed for Martin's money, as the small group made their way to the rooms near the ship, Jacob quickly raised his weapon and placed it next to the robber's temple. This was serious and everyone who stood nearby knew that justice would be quick. The potential robber fell back in fear and disappeared into the crowd. Martin held Martha to his chest to slow her trembling. Etta's teenagers in the group were impressed. A lesson for their lives. The seven travelers found an open door that suggested there were rooms for rent. They followed the proprietor to their room giving him three Deutschmarks, one for each day they planned to stay. The proprietor offered no response, took the money, and pointed to a door. Martin cautiously went to the door and slowly opened it. On the floor lay several mattresses filled with straw and covered with a dirty cloth. Probably full of bedbugs. This was the best they could do, and he knew it.

There was no place to wash. The water smelled of waste. The outhouses were near the end of the dock to allow for human waste to fall into the harbor. The noise throughout the night was continuous. Sea breezes were cool. Gulls circled and screamed as they fought for scraps of food. The days of waiting were long and the docks were filled with danger.

As the three days passed, the confinement made the room smell even more. However, there was still a feeling of relief. On the third day the small group held tight to their belongings and moved toward the *California*.

CHAPTER 10

THE ATLANTIC

THE SATHOFFS AND THE SCHREADERS huddled together as they now moved toward the visible gangplank. It seemed as if they had been together for decades. Their expressions and movements all seemed to show sincere care for each member of the tiny group. They stayed together as Etta was the first to step on the slippery boards that led to the main decks. She squeezed the railings tightly and held her few possessions in the opposite hand. She was followed by her children and then by the Schreaders. Martin was the last and made sure that all members of the group were safely onboard.

Immigrants without money were directed toward the steerage section of the ship. Strange smells were everywhere; the hallways were dark. Etta and her four children were given a cabin in the lowest section of the ship. Martin and Martha were five doors away from them. The small rooms were remarkably clean. Washing facilities would have to be shared. The rooms were made from steel with one small light attached to the middle of the ceiling. Since there were no switches, the light remained on at all times. Each group settled into their rooms with their small number of belongings. Boarding was completed.

The passengers in steerage were allowed to ascend to the main deck where they could watch the ship depart the harbor. A small meal of cornbread mush would be served in a large cafeteria just off the ship's kitchen. The boarding planks were removed and the heavy ropes binding the ship to the dock were loosened. The few passengers from the area waved their hands as the ship began its departure. A small group on the dock consisting mostly of mothers, fathers, brothers and sisters were waving goodbye. They would probably no longer be part of their passenger's future.

The sidewheel began to show its power as the pistons reacted to the pressure from the hot steam. The men in the coal bins shoveled the black material into the fire boxes that heated the boilers. They were shirtless and covered with sweat mixed with coal dust. The ship loaded with nearly two hundred souls began to crunch and heave. It had been making this trip for nearly twenty years. It was as if it were embracing and comforting the anxious immigrants hoping for a new and better life. The experienced crew answered the many questions put forth to them by their passengers. Many languages were spoken. The names, ages and origins of each passenger were entered into the log of the ship and saved for all time.

After the warm meal, many passengers returned to their cabins and collapsed into an exhausted sleep. Those who could remain awake stayed on the main deck throughout portions of the night as the flickering lights on shore began to dim to nothing. The final spots of land appeared on the starboard side. The land and the lights soon disappeared as they moved into open water. The final visible village was named Brunsbuttel, for most on board the ship, this meant goodbye forever. The tiny scenes were captured and preserved in the memories of those who remained awake.

The Ocean was cold. Large waves rocked the ship from side to side. Adapting oneself to the rocking motion was simply not possible as the waves seemed to have no consistency in their size and direction. Walking on the deck was difficult for Martha, so she held tightly to the railings working hard to prevent a serious fall that might hurt the baby she was carrying. She did know that the rocking of the ship would doom her to spending most of the next three weeks lying on her back in a tiny room near the bottom of the ship. She did try to keep herself looking nice by combing her hair and maintaining a positive and happy outlook.

Try as she might, she hated to look at herself in the tiny mirror available in her room. Physical hygiene was nearly impossible because fresh water was scarce. Washing clothes was not an easy task for only small amounts of water would be made available briefly two times during the three-week voyage. There were no facilities for bathing. The only available fresh water was used for cooking and drinking. Any other use was not a priority.

Martha suffered. Thoughts of a new home in Mobridge, South Dakota, provided little relief. As the boat rocked in the North Sea and eventually moved to the North Atlantic, seasickness was everywhere. Pails and bags with vomit lined the narrow hallways. The ocean swells neared twenty feet. Martha was immensely uncomfortable. She vowed to persevere and dreamed of the new home for her baby. Martin's head pounded with surging headaches and a tender stomach. This felt like a trip into hell. Three weeks seemed like eternity.

As the days passed, Martin made his way to the deck and observed that the Atlantic Ocean was simply an immense expanse of nothing but water. He looked for ships in the distance and found none. What he did not know was that the ocean is not flat. The curvature of the earth makes objects on the water disappear at about twelve miles.

At the midpoint of the Atlantic between London and New

York, passenger ships passed near the ice floes from the nearby land mass of Greenland. The captain with much experience maneuvered the ship through the blocks of ice keeping his crew and passengers safe. The *California* was on this same route as the great ship, *Titanic*, which made its disastrous maiden voyage twelve years later. That voyage would never be completed. The engineers and nautical experts in Belfast, Ireland, were already drawing the outlines of this great vessel which would be the largest and fastest ship of its time.

If it were not for the discomfort, one would consider the days almost boring. Each day the horizon seemed to flow into eternity. Would the trip ever end? As the voyage neared its conclusion, Martin was able to see a tiny speck in the distance off the bow. Not believing his eyes, he asked one of the crew what he was seeing. The attendant could not speak German and did not understand. He said something in English. The tiny spot grew larger. Martin became more excited and asked others if they were also seeing the spot. Finally, a German speaking woman touched Martin's hand and smiled.

She said, "That is your new home. You are looking at the Statue of Liberty." Her eyes filled with tears.

With excitement, Martin jumped and hollered and ran into the lower level of the ship to find Martha. He wanted to share his joy and help Martha find hers. Martha was excited but not for the same reason. She wanted to get off the ship because her seasickness had made her extremely miserable.

She said to herself, "I will never go on one of these things again." This was a promise that she would easily be able to keep.

Martin and Martha slowly made their way to the main deck of the ship. The statue was larger now and the approaching city was also becoming rapidly clearer.

The lady again said, "That is the Statue of Liberty donated by the country of France to their friends in America five years ago."

The ship's passengers did not know that the statue created by the French sculptor, Frederic-Auguste Barthold, was modeled in the image of his mother.

As the ship passed the statue, its presence grew many times taller than the ship. The lady told Martin and Martha that a plaque consisting of two short sentences is located on the pedestal of the great statue. It said, "Give me your tired, your poor, your huddled masses yearning to breathe free, the wretched refuse of your teeming shores, those, the homeless, tempest-tossed to me. I lift my lamp beside the golden door."

The author, Emma Lazarus, was just in her twenties and also an immigrant like the newly arriving couple on the ship. She wrote the engravings for the plaque just one year earlier.

CHAPTER 11

ELLIS ISLAND

THE SHIP PASSED THE STATUE on the port side, opposite the paddlewheel. The hope was that each immigrant would have a memory that would be with them till the day they died. Passing the Statue of Liberty not only gave those on the ship a sense of relief but also a growing anxiety about what lay ahead of each of them as they started their new lives.

Martha and Martin looked toward the large dock and the huge cement building just beyond. The building was surrounded by an iron fence with large steel gates. It seemed as though they might be gazing on a prison. Directions from the ship's crew were firm as the gangplanks were being moved up to the ship. People who were already citizens could freely leave the ship passing through simple customs. The remaining one-hundred and fifty-nine souls were steered rather forcefully to the gangplank that led to the large cement building with the steel gates.

One young man had died during the trip. His body was rapidly removed and taken to a section of the building where an examination could be done in order to discover either foul play or contagious disease. His journey would end in the Potters Field of New York. If there was enough information on him or within his belongings, a short note would be sent to relatives back in his home country.

The remaining passengers moved on the long slippery plank to the gated guard rooms on shore. They were immediately given instructions as to what they could expect and how they should behave. Immigrants believed to be carrying disease of some type were immediately returned to the ship for the voyage back to Europe. All others entered the building to the sound of excited and anxious echoes of voices reverberating throughout the large room.

The big room had a twenty-foot ceiling with fifteen-foot windows above their heads. The sorting began immediately. People believed to have a temporary contagious illness were immediately placed in quarantine. Martin and Martha were allowed to move along. Health staff marveled at Martha's condition. The intense penetrating odors from the ship were everywhere in the sparkling clean building.

People were given pencil and paper tests in an effort to prevent people who were retarded or had other mental problems. People of color were given special examinations without explanation. Everyone was interviewed intensely by immigration personnel in an attempt to discover if each person would be able to leave the loyalty to their former nation behind and develop a new loyalty to their new country. Loyalty to the new nation needed to be established. This process was not difficult for the immigrants because they were frequently leaving a nation where the government was not considered friendly to its people. They did not feel loyal to their former country. They would willingly pledge their loyalty to their new country.

Each passenger had to clarify their purpose for being in the United States and where they intended to settle. Nearly all of them were farmers who would settle somewhere in the center of the nation. Martin and Martha stated their intent was to go to Mobridge, South Dakota where Martin had a cousin. Etta Sathoff and her children would be settling with her brother and family in Parkersburg, Iowa.

Finally, all the entrance paperwork was finished, so they all would be heading for the great train station built by Cornelius Vanderbilt nearly fifty years earlier. Their travels would take them to an American city called Chicago, population 800,000. This would be called the Northern route of the Great Northern Railroad as it made its way to the West Coast through Mobridge, South Dakota. Etta and her family would board the train with Martin and Martha for the ride to Chicago where they would say goodbye because Etta and her children would be taking the Southern route of the railroad to the city of Burlington, Iowa. Each family was given a one-way ticket on a trolley that would leave Castle Garden (the South end of Manhattan) to the great railroad station.

The city was strange and the streets were crowded much like the docks of Homburg. Homburg seemed to be in the distant past but it was only thirty days ago that they were in that German city. Horses jammed the streets of New York and the smell of manure was everywhere. People cursed, peddled their wares and shopped. New York City felt like a massive ant hill. Martha thought that there must be some organization behind this turbulent chaos. There seemed to be no end.

For nearly two hours the families made their way to Grand Central Station, a building that seemed to have the appearance of a great cathedral. Its spires were topped by gargoyles. Roman scenes and murals were carved in wood and stone that showed all the colors of the rainbow. Its frontage was sparkling and beautiful as it seemed to lend an order of majesty amid the noise and confusion surrounding it.

The trolley finally stopped and the hopeful travelers took their belongings and walked into the large building. The halls and walls were filled with instructions on how to find a correct train for the final leg of their journey. In addition to the permanent features of the building there were pictures of men with big muscles in small outfits which covered little of their bodies. The travelers were observing pictures of bodybuilders which had become a rage in America. Martha was not sure if she should be noticing these men who seemed to have little modesty.

There was a small kiosk in the building that had a sign that read "Instructions for German-speaking People." Their faces immediately erupted with smiles. It was uplifting to find others that seemed to understand the last month of travel. Instructions were given and the seven enlightened individuals moved toward their trains.

Martha could now feel the kicks of the baby regularly. Basic life activities such as walking became more difficult. They were told that when the large clock reached 5:30 PM they would see a train that would be traveling west to a city called Erie. They were to be in the seventh hallway at that time. After finding their way to the hallway, they rested on the hard-wooden bench to wait for the train. The train arrived at 4:15 PM. It was identified as going west to the city of Erie, Pennsylvania. All instructions were given in English.

The German couple were beginning to recognize the tone of voice that suggested something was about to happen. The train paused for nearly one-half hour for boarding. The smell of horse manure was now being replaced by the smells of burning coal and grease. Martin and Martha quickly found seats for the next leg of their journey.

The wait for the train to move was short as the big machine began to exert force on the cars as it pulled from the station. The train moved through the city gathering speed and soon passed into the beautiful green countryside. The trees, fields and farms reminded them of the beloved homeland they had just left.

CHAPTER 12

ACROSS AMERICA

For the first time in nearly seven weeks, the young couple was given a chance to relax and sit on something that had a soft cushion. With the new comfort there was a heightened awareness that there was a small human being growing in Martha's body. Martin frequently placed his hand on her stomach to feel the tiny movements as the little one attempted to find comfort. This put a broad smile on Martha's face for the first time since the beginning thoughts of this adventure.

They both felt a freedom from the restrictive laws that had governed them in the past. Although, they could not speak any of the language in this new country, there was a feeling that they had just found a new homeland. Martin thought he could fight for this new country should it ever be required. Their eyes filled with tears as they held hands. They were facing the whole world with not much understanding and a great deal of love.

The train moved in what seemed like a breakneck speed of forty miles per hour as it traveled through the New Jersey countryside and on to the hills of Pennsylvania. Small farms began to appear with some plants and a few animals. One-hundred-year-old log homes were everywhere. Occasionally, Martin saw children playing in yards and on the porches of their homes. He wanted someday to have one of those homes for his soon-to-be wife and little baby. The train traveled through the night and arrived as the sun was coming up on a small village on Lake Erie called Erie, Pennsylvania.

This community would become known as the only city in America that had a positive balance of trade with China in the year 2010. Erie, Pennsylvania manufactures the best diesel engines in the world, so the demand for this product is high everywhere in the world.

The stop was short. Martha felt rested which was the first time she was able to get comfortable as the train rumbled and rocked through the Pennsylvania countryside. The only distraction was the kicking of the baby. She had already noticed an intense love for the little one that she believed she would be meeting in about two months.

During the daylight of the second day, the train stopped in the city of Cleveland, Ohio. The stop there was longer and the conductor suggested that people leave the train for a while to use the facilities at the railroad station and perhaps eat some food, if they had some money. After a refreshing stop, the train left the Cleveland station heading for Toledo, Ohio. Martin felt certain that his destination in South Dakota would have the same beauty as the Ohio countryside.

He noticed that most little towns that they passed through had small train stations. In a curious manner he asked another German speaking passenger on the train this question. The other passenger who also spoke some English did not know the answer. He then turned to waiter on the train the question in broken English. The waiter was black and was the first black person Martin had ever seen.

"Why so many small cities by the tracks?" Questioned the man.

The waiter answered in German, "Each village is located twelve miles from the other because that is the length of time that it would take for a farmer to bring produce to the railhead and return to his home in a single day. These little towns are called 'jerk waters.'"

Martha was surprised to hear the waiter speak German, so she asked him, "Why do they call them such a funny name?"

The waiter had learned some German since German-speaking people had been asking him questions in in their native language for the past twenty years. He simply had to learn some German to be able to answer their questions.

He said, "As the mighty train travels through and slows at each town, it gathers mail from the citizens of the village and also jerks water from a trough located near the track. This adds to the water supply in the main boiler for making additional steam. Bringing the train to a complete stop simply required too much energy to again start the massive forward movement."

Martha smiled and nodded her approval.

The train continued onto the great hub city of Chicago, population nearing 800,000. They moved past Lake Michigan and through the giant stockyards of South Chicago and on to Central Station. They also saw smelting units that processed iron ore from the vast discoveries in northern Minnesota. Meat and grain processing plants filled the air with smells. Agricultural products were everywhere. Martin dreamed of a beautiful, successful farm and someday, shipping his produce to this great city. Martha dreamed of a white house with a porch and happy children.

The two families rented rooms for an overnight stay. The rooms offered a tub for cleaning and washing clothes. This effort took most of the evening but spirits were high, perhaps better than they had ever been. Beginning the next day, the families would split with the Sathoff family taking the Southern track of the Union Pacific to Davenport, Iowa. They would then take the North spur to the community of Waterloo where they would meet Etta's brother.

The Schreader family would take the North track of the Milwaukee Road to Minneapolis, Minnesota. They would then continue their journey through western Minnesota to Mobridge, South Dakota.

The Schreader's would begin to travel the next morning. Their expectation was that it would take about two days before arriving at their final destination. Martin was exploding with excitement and anticipation.

During the night while slowing rolling through Minneapolis, Martha noticed that the baby was not kicking. It seemed to her as if the fetus had gone to sleep. After leaving Minneapolis, the train rolled on through Willmar, Minnesota, through Ortonville, Minnesota, and on to Aberdeen, South Dakota. Martha was in a cold sweat wondering when the baby might kick again. She did not reveal her heightened anxiety to Martin.

When they were about forty minutes east of a tiny South Dakota town called Bristol, Martha began to feel painful contractions.

With a controlled voice, Martha said, "Martin help me, I think the baby is coming."

Martin reacted as if Martha had asked him to eat a full-grown tree. Then he said loudly in German, "Is there a doctor on the train?"

The passengers stared in bewilderment as a lady of character and style sitting between two neatly dressed little girls stood and said in German, "I will help you."

She moved with confidence to the front of the car and instructed Martha to lie on the floor. The rocking train made it difficult to maintain balance without grasping the seat rails. By now Martha was screaming in pain. The baby was demanding to be born.

The lady said in a calm voice, "My name is Edith, and I am going to help you."

Martha screamed, "Is my baby all right?"

Edith did not speak as she assisted with the painful delivery. In a community with no doctor, Edith had served as a midwife many times. She moved confidently helping the now dead fetus through the birth canal. Her beautiful dress was covered with the liquids associated with childbirth.

Martin stood white with terror. Edith cut the umbilical cord of the tiny baby girl and placed the infant on a small cloth near her eldest daughter. They wrapped it fully. Martha cried uncontrollably, her heart ached in a way that words could not describe. Between muffled sobs she would give out a muffled groan of pain. The train continued to move. The passengers were silent and somewhat frozen in their movements and expressions.

Edith spoke, "I live in the next town, Bristol. My husband is the German Lutheran pastor there. We must get off the train. You may stay in our home for a few days until you feel well enough to continue your journey."

Martin stood weeping without words as Edith held Martha's hand. She said, "You must remain on the floor until the train stops in Bristol."

Since Bristol was small, the train did not ordinarily stop. However, since Edith commanded respect, the engineer had made for allowances.

While Martha lay on the floor she felt hopeless and vulnerable. Edith cleaned her so that they could make the short drive to the pastor's home. She knew that her husband would be at the station to help. She also knew that her husband had provided love and care for many families in the Bristol area who had lost children or simply loved ones. She also hoped that Martha and Martin would never suffer a loss like this again in their lives.

Pastor Walter was waiting at the station and was hoping for a joyous reunion. Edith and her daughters had been gone for three weeks visiting her sister in St. Paul. Edith's expression immediately informed him that there would be no festivities this evening. She handed the forever lost child to Walter. Going back into the train, she and Martin gently helped Martha to her feet. She gave a glance to her girls that required no words. She also thought, as she looked at her children, that she needed to thank God for their presence and beauty.

Edith and Martin firmly held Martha as she stumbled toward the waiting wagon feeling drainage from her body. The children silently followed while Pastor Walter gently set the baby's body near one side of the small wagon. Edith placed coats on the wagon floor and helped Martha to lay flat. Pastor Walter drove the wagon with his two little girls at his side. Edith, with dignity and strength walked behind the wagon with Martin at her side. He shook and stumbled along grateful for the help of these strangers.

The journey to the parsonage took fifteen minutes. By now everyone was physically and emotionally exhausted. They helped Martha to her feet and up the three steps into the living room of the home. Edith grabbed towels and placed them on the sofa. Martha stumbled toward the sofa and laid her tired body down. For a brief moment, each person attempted to gain some composure so that Martha and Martin could begin their lives again without their little treasure.

Edith started the wood stove and began to heat water for the tub so Martha would be able to clean herself. Martha had never seen a tub for bathing in her whole life. She was numbed by the rapid changes going on around her. Edith went to her closet and found clean clothes for Martha in an attempt to help her regain her dignity from this horrible trauma.

The families prayed together. The pain of this loss would last forever. Martha remained alone in one room while dinner was being prepared in the kitchen. Pastor Walter discussed with Martin what needed be done over the next several days.

Over the evening meal, Pastor Walter learned that Martin and Martha were Catholic. He suggested that Father Jonas be invited to come and plan a funeral service. The burial would take place in St. Aloysius Catholic Church Cemetery in Bristol. The mortician from Aberdeen would be notified to come and prepare the body for burial. The trip from Aberdeen was twenty-five miles so the notification to him would need to be done by a telegraph. If they sent the telegraph immediately the next morning, the mortician could arrive by midday the next day.

While these plans were being made Martha asked Martin and those present to come into the living room. She had something to say.

"I want my child to be named for my beloved grandmother, Elizabeth."

All agreed.

Father Jonas noted that the couple was not married and asked, "Would like me to perform your marriage ceremony?"

After a brief surprise there were smiles of assent. The wedding ceremony would take place on the cemetery grounds near the grave of their beloved little Elizabeth.

Bristol, South Dakota, would remain part of their lives as long as they would live. During these tense and grieving times, the world had changed forever for Martin and Martha. The dignified and caring Edith stood by Martha to give her support. The style and confidence that Edith exhibited would live within Martha for the remainder of her years.

Several days passed in the warm, caring atmosphere of the pastor's home. The bed was soft and comfortable allowing the emotional and physical healing to begin. Martin and Martha were preparing for the end of their journey one hundred and twenty miles to the west.

They once again boarded the giant machine that puffed pillars of white smoke as it rumbled along the tracks. It was taking them to their destiny. As Martin again gazed from the train window he noticed that the beautiful greenery of the past nearly one thousand miles had disappeared. There were fewer trees, poorer crops in the fields, little greenery, and lots of wind. His heart began to sink.

Five hours later he stepped off the train and looked into the smiling face of his cousin. Everything in his presence seemed to be empty and without hope. They moved their few things into the rough bunkhouse that was usually inhabited by cowboys who took care of the range cattle. The buffalo herds had now all been hunted and depleted.

In the days that followed Martin, and occasionally Martha, explored the small community located on the beautiful Missouri River. The white people that inhabited the area were a tough, seemingly embattled group which was a personality that they did not understand. Almost all of the activities in the town centered around the movement of cattle.

The saloon appeared to be the heart of the community. It seemed that everyone had a handgun or a rifle. Men were tall and skinny with wrinkled skin from many hours exposed to the hot sun. Most had a cigarette with a long ash hanging from their lips. Martin and Martha noticed very few women. This town seemed very foreign and unwelcoming to the young couple.

CHAPTER 13

MAKING A HOME

MARTIN AND MARTHA HAD KNOWN EXTREME POVERTY and hopelessness in Germany. This cattle town seemed to have similar qualities to their German village with the familiar rundown buildings, broken doors and abandoned pieces of equipment. The difference appeared to be that the people did not seem to be attached to a larger family system which was something that they had taken for granted in their homeland. The cowboys did not seem to be attached to generations of parents and grandparents. There seemed to be no attachments and only fleeting friendships that surrounded local saloons. There were several prostitutes who also inhabited the saloons.

Children seemed as scarce as the women. With no children there were no schools to set examples. The people were loud and frequently fought. They looked at Martha without being sure of what her presence meant. Marriages were few and not well understood. From the first days of their arrival this young couple had grave doubts about a place where few people had common values and understandings.

This became much clearer on a late August morning. The cattle had been fed and the horses were tied and supplies were ready for future days. Martha was near the bunkhouse doing the daily chores outside to avoid the inside odors. Martin mopped his brow and gazed at the very large railroad bridge that the trains used to cross the Missouri River. There were no trains scheduled at this time, and he was curious to know what was on the other side of the river.

He pulled himself onto the tracks and began to take steps from tie-to-tie heading for the other side. After walking almost a quarter of a mile, he began to reach the other side. It looked as if he had walked into another world. The people, the buildings and the style of the environment was very different from his small town on the other side of the river. As he got closer to the other side, he stumbled a bit because he was tired from maintaining his balance for so long. He looked up. Coming toward him was a young man who was not quite an adult nor was he a child. The young man's hair was long and black and was put up in braids that hung over each shoulder. His skin was dark and slightly rutted from spending much time in the sun.

Martin was greeted by this young man with a rage filled stare followed by a shout in another language. The young man stood firm. Martin froze. The young man stood firm and again shouted. Seconds passed like hours. Martin's eyes were fixed on the figure before him. Slowly he looked beyond the young man and saw a much older man with similar braided hair graced by three feathers.

The older man's face and posture clearly communicated to Martin that any step forward might be dangerous. The man with the feathers cradled a lever action rifle. The older man made no attempt to use the rifle. However, he left the impression with Martin that he could use it effectively. The older man again shouted in an unknown language and pointed across the river to the east. The message was clear in any language — "Go back!"

With a mix of anxiety and fear, Martin slowly and cautiously turned with his back to the angry older man and

Making a Home

began to trace his steps back toward the east and over the bridge. He noticed as he turned to go that there was a strange object with bright colors and carvings off on his right. He had never seen a pole like this. He was frightened. He took little time to examine the object that stood approximately two hundred feet in the near distance.

Re-crossing the railroad bridge seemed to take an eternity. The pine tar smell from the timbers below filled his nostrils. He slipped, landing face-down on the timbers staring at the river one hundred and fifty feet below. Finally, after reaching the east bank of the Missouri River, he immediately went to the small bunkhouse where he shared his experience with Martha. His voice was both vigorous and anxious. Martha seemed confused. She had no frame of reference to understand what had happened.

Amid their confusion, they decided to ask Cousin Abe if he knew what had just happened to Martin and tell him what that colorful pole meant. They were somewhat irritated that no one had told them of the possible danger so close by. To the best of his understanding, Abe stated that for the past century white Americans had waged war and taken lands from the native people who had lived there for centuries. He did his best to explain that Martin should never cross the bridge again. The Indians who lived across the river were dangerous.

Abe explained that on the other side of the river was the Standing Rock Indian Reservation, a piece of earth the size of the state of Rhode Island. It was probably the driest place within hundreds of miles. The white government of the United States had decided that this was where Native Americans should live.

The strange pole with the painted faces marked the grave of Sitting Bull, an Indian chief who was much loved by the

Native American people of the Dakotas. Sitting Bull had been slain just five years earlier. Although he had been murdered by one of his own, the Native American people strongly believed that it was the manipulation of the Indian agents that caused his death.

Abe said, "The Indians at Standing Rock will never be able to forgive us for the death of Sitting Bull. You were definitely in danger after crossing that bridge."

Martin's face was blank as he stared intently at Abe. As they turned and walked away from Abe, Martha's face was filled with tears of fear.

She said, "We cannot stay here. I am afraid. This land is no good for anything. I want to leave now."

Martin wondered out loud, "Where can we go?"

Deep within Martin's soul, he felt as if his trust in Abe had been violated. This was not what he expected when he came to Mobridge to work with Abe on his ranch.

Martin and Martha dialogued through the evening searching for a solution. This land was strange and options were few. Martha remained anxious but more determined to leave this place. They had to think of something. Several years prior a family who had a similar experience left this hot, empty place and took a thirteen-hundred-mile journey to a small place called Lakeview, Canada, now named Provost. Abe, who saw the fear in Martha's eyes, told the young couple that he had heard of this place in Canada. He said he had heard that this place did have small wheat farms, chickens and milking cows and seemed like a much friendlier place.

Somehow Martin and Martha felt this new place in Canada must be close to heaven.

CHAPTER 14

TRAVELING TO CANADA

Still suffering from the disappointment with their move to Mobridge, they looked with caution upon this new idea of starting over once again in Canada as the place that might fulfill their dreams. Yet they had decided that remaining in Mobridge was unthinkable, so in late August, Martin repaired an old wagon for the upcoming journey. He purchased two old horses that he was sure could make the trip to their new home. Martha was quite familiar with the lack of comfort that would come with riding in a wagon for such a long distance. This would be nearly twice as long as her previous ride. There were no cities along the way but instead small villages with names like: Williston, Glasgow, Shelby and Medicine Hat.

Lakeview, Canada, was a small village of about one hundred people located in the central regions of the Canadian province called Alberta. It was about one hundred miles south and east of a larger city called Edmonton. Again, blessed with high hopes for a more pleasant future, the young couple turned the horse and the wagon toward the northwest. They now considered becoming citizens of another new nation, a much less settled one.

For the first hours Martha sat quietly on the bouncing seat

of the wooden wagon with steel rims. She could see for miles. Sounds occasionally distracted her thoughts. The iron wheels bounced among the stones to the rhythm of the pounding horses' feet. Her thoughts remained in the community that she had just left even though the stay in Mobridge lasted only the ten weeks. She spent many hours on that rough ride toward Canada reflecting on her time in Mobridge.

She constantly thought how vulnerable she had been to the tall leather faced cowboys with wrinkled skin and handmade cigarettes hanging from their mouths who seemed to be everywhere in that town. She reflected on how they watched her when she left the bunkhouse to do her chores. When they spoke to her, it was clear that it was not about friendship and more about looking for a victim. That look terrified her. She was sure that she would not be safe when Martin was gone on cattle drives for over a month. Each time those cattle drives approached, her anxiety grew.

Mobridge had very few women who lived in that cattle town. She had only met two, Eva and Catherine. Both worked at the saloon. Martha guessed that they were in their mid-thirties. The other ladies whom she had seen were older and married to older men who seemed to be town leaders. While Martin worked in the corrals, Martha was able to talk to some of the older women on occasion. Conversations were brief but would often drift to female safety when husbands were gone. Because of the stories the women told her, Martha was sure that she must do something. She just didn't know what to do.

Martha, in the absence of women her own age, befriended the two ladies at the saloon. They were kind and offered her conversation and warmth. Catherine and Eva revealed that they had no families and worked for the pleasure of the saloon owner and surrounding cowboys. Martha was bewildered by this arrangement. Conversations grew more serious as the ladies from the saloon began to reveal their concern for this woman who spoke little English. Without specifically telling Martha what they did for a living, Martha began to realize that these two friends gained their living by providing sexual favors to the many unattached roving men in the area. This revelation surprised and shocked Martha, but she liked both Eva and Catherine. She decided to overlook their occupations and simply accept their friendship without judgment.

As the conversations grew more personal, her two friends explained that there used to be three of them who worked at the saloon. Jessie, their other friend, died this past month from complications as a result of an abortion. It was also revealed that most of the unmarried residents of the community had venereal diseases of one type or another.

Martha realized that without Martin nearby she would be in serious danger for her health and even perhaps her life. Questioning the older married ladies, Martha began to realize the sad fate of many young women in this area. The older ladies indicated that it was common practice for people that worked for the railroad to entice girls from the streets of Milwaukee to come to South Dakota to seek a fortune. The only physical protection afforded these vulnerable young girls was from the tavern owner who was a disinterested onlooker most times.

Each girl had to purchase a small single shot twenty-two caliber pistol that she carried at all times. She had to keep it within easy reach if it were going to offer even a modicum of protection. After several of these conversations, Martha realized that she would most certainly need to begin to look after her own safety, as well as, relying on Martin. The sheriff could handle such matters as bank robbery and horse thievery, but the sexual safety of a young woman did not ride high on his list of concerns.

As the stories from Eva and Catherine and the older women whom she had spoken with became more troublesome, she realized that she had to begin providing for her own protection. Besides thinking about leaving this area, she began to devise other mechanisms for trying to stay safe. She started discarding her clothing that suggested femininity. Anything with lace and frills was packed away. She cut her hair short and began to wear boots and trousers. She hoped this attire would attract less attention. At a more personal moment in a quiet conversation with her young friends, Eva reached under her mattress and displayed a six shot Colt 45 revolver.

Eva said, "I want you to have this, and I will teach you to shoot with confidence. I have extra shells for practice."

Martha stared at the gun. It seemed so big and scary. "Where will I carry such a huge gun?"

"Sew a place in your shawl that will hold the gun and always keep it with you. Never leave it," Eva intoned.

"A cowboy once left the gun with me before a trail ride, and he never came back. You may keep it. He taught me to shoot it before he left, so I can teach you."

"Thank you, Eva,"

In her heart, Martha knew that the love she felt for her husband was beyond description. She also knew that Martin was a gentle man who tended to trust people in situations that terrified her. She was not convinced that he could handle a desperate situation, so she felt that she must shoulder the banner of strength for their family.

Before falling asleep, Martha would frequently let her mind drift to thoughts of Edith, the preacher's wife. Her dignity her style and self-assurance were remarkable. In the same thought, she also admired Eva and Catherine, who had shown her love, courage and concern despite their sad and desperate occupation. Her short-lived interactions with these three women began to help her form opinions and ideas on what she wanted to become, and how she wanted to conduct herself.

Bouncing over a large dip in the dirt road jolted Martha's thoughts back to the present and to the long journey she had just begun. Martin sat proudly by his new wife with no idea how much she had changed since leaving the small village in Germany, only four months ago. The wagon easily contained their few possessions. Their food consisted of fifty pounds of cornmeal and a large block of cured bacon. Additional food would have to be found along the seven hundred and twenty-two-mile trip that would take approximately forty-five days.

On nights when there was no nearby farms or villages, they would have to sleep on the hard boards of the wagon. They were always on the lookout for small streams and rivers to water the horses and clean their clothing. Army posts were the most desirable places for their overnight stays. The Calvary officers usually allowed people to have small rooms and eat in the soldier's mess. They were always good sources for information that would help the travelers find the best routes to the new locations. This part of the United States had undeveloped roads with mostly dirt trails with ruts and mud.

The first day they headed to a small town called Mound City, South Dakota, population forty. This town was known as a burial ground for the Mandan tribe of Indians that inhabited the area. Burial mounds were everywhere. When the locals noticed that someone was passing through, they made no effort to help or assist in any way because they had been exploited in the past making them wary of strangers passing through. After the exhausting first day of travel, Martin and Martha had to sleep on the hard boards of the wagon fully exposed to any danger that might be lurking in the town.

Martha remembered the advice from Eva, so she kept the Colt forty-five by her side all night long.

From Mound City, their travels took them to Mandan, North Dakota. They would spend the night at the cavalry post called Fort Lincoln where the uninhabited home of the bellicose cavalry general, George Armstrong Custer was located. Mandan had already earned the nickname, "Where the West begins."

A few of the soldiers were German immigrants, so they were able to help Martin and Martha navigate the language barrier. The young travelers were overjoyed to find people who spoke German and could answer their many questions about the travels to come. Post personnel provided for the needs of the two travelers. The soldiers were anxious to hear stories of their travels since many of them were from the East and had not been home in many years. Those from Germany asked many questions about the homeland. After a hearty evening meal, the group enjoyed lively conversation filled with laughter.

After returning to their room, Martha thought, "I feel safe here. I wish we could stay longer."

"I wish we could too, Martha," replied Martin. "But winter weather would soon be here, and we must get to Lakeville before it snows."

They left Fort Lincoln as the sun rose and headed for a town called Underwood, North Dakota, population three hundred. The railroad had not yet arrived but would be there in eight years. While passing near the town, a group of young men between the ages of about eighteen to twenty-four approached the wagon. Martin brought the horses pulling the slow-moving vehicle to a halt. At first the faces were friendly; however, they gradually grew fierce as they demanded money and the tiny number of possessions in the wagon. They also shared a penetrating look at Martha.

As usual, Martin tried to help them understand his situation feeling that if he remained accommodating speaking to them kindly, they would be understanding in return. The young marauders did not speak German and could not understand Martin's heavily accented English. Instead of reacting more civilly to the young travelers, they became more belligerent.

This was the event that Martha feared would happen to them. She sat motionless and innocent as she slipped her hand into the waistband of her dress and firmly gripped the revolver's handle. She waited. The situation grew more tense. Realizing that this situation required a different kind of understanding, she took the loaded weapon from her waistband and pointed it directly at the head of the young man who seemed to be the leader. She said nothing. Expressions on the faces of the young men immediately changed, the boy who appeared the most aggressive, stood still as did his friends. They looked wide-eyed at the big revolver as they turned and ran in the opposite direction.

Martin looked at Martha in shock and awe. "Where did you get that gun?"

"My friend, Eva, gave it to me in Mobridge. She taught me to shoot it, so we would be protected in our travels."

Martin again started the horses moving while he smiled and shook his head marveling at Martha's revelation. The little wagon turned north and west as they continued their journey. The land was barren with dust swirling through the small brush. They spotted a butte in the distance which provided a guide for direction because the path that they were on was not heavily traveled.

The wagon slid in and out of the ruts always reminding its passengers that it was a good idea to hang tightly to the seat. Martin held the reins with one hand and the seat with the other. He did this until his back ached.

They finally arrived at a place called Newtown which was a tribal headquarters for the Mandan, Hidatsa and the Arikara nations. This community was peaceful with Indians and settlers milling about together. The Indian agent at the trading post was helpful and did speak a little German. He also could understand Martin's heavily accented English so was able to answer their questions. Martin and Martha felt safe and were able to gather much collective wisdom from the native people and settlers who milled about the trading post.

After spending most of a day at Newtown gathering additional supplies, the little wagon headed toward a small village with a big future called Williston. Fort Buford was close to Williston which provided for an atmosphere of security. Williston was also the site for the confluence of the Yellowstone and Missouri rivers.

Traveling the next day, the couple passed into Wolf Point, Montana, near Fort Peck and another Indian reservation. Again, they found the night secure, and the next morning they went on to a Scottish settlement called Glascow, Montana.

Traveling on, they eventually arrived in Saco, Montana. A place that got its name by having some town officials spin a world globe on its axis while a blindfolded resident pointed to a spot on it. When the others looked at where he had touched the globe with his finger, it was on Saco, Maine. They then decided that the name of their small town would become Saco, Montana.

They crossed into Canada at Wild Horse and traveled on to a strangely named village called Medicine Hat. Native Americans gathered in this Indian village for conversation and understanding. The medicine men who gathered in this location shared stories and experiences in an effort to improve their craft. They all had a similar arrangement of feathers in their hair to signify to the native people that they were medicine men. The feather arrangement in their hair was called a medicine hat, and the Canadian community which grew from this gathering of native people became known as Medicine Hat.

The native people were kind and supportive of Martha and Martin. They helped prepare the young travelers for the remaining part of their journey to the farming settlement known as Lakeview. This small community consisted of ten small log homes haphazardly arranged by its citizens.

CHAPTER 15

MARTIN AND MARTHA'S NEW HOME

WHEN THEY ARRIVED IN LAKEVIEW, Martin noticed a man attending to his horse and said to him. "I would like to find the cabin belonging to Emil and Nina Hammerstien." The horseman smiled and pointed to a small log home with a spiral of smoke emerging from its chimney. He said, "They are waiting for you."

Martin drove the wagon two hundred feet to the front door of the Hammerstien cabin. He cautiously slid down from the hard wagon seat to the ground and walked the ten steps to the door. He looked over his shoulder with a hopeful smile as Martha waited on the wagon. Still uncertain as to what he might find, Martin gently knocked on the door.

A large woman with a broad smile opened the door. Nina had been expecting him as she looked over his shoulder toward the wagon where Martha was sitting. She was quickly joined by her husband, Emil, who greeted Martin warmly. Nina went to the wagon to help Martha down from her perch. Together they walked to the small cabin where food and warmth awaited them. Emil and Nina wanted to celebrate the arrival of the newcomers by inviting her two sons and one daughter-in-law to have dinner with them that evening.

Martin would be Emil's employee helping run the farm. Emil and Nina were successful farmers in their mid-sixties.

Their farming operation had been very successful over the past twenty years, but Emil's health was beginning to hinder his ability to perform all the tasks necessary to maintain the farm. He needed help from a younger man, so he was very happy to see Martin and realize his strength combined with a gentleness would be a great asset.

This small gathering was joined by the Hammerstien's two sons, Jacob and Andrew who were in their mid to late thirties. The boys also had successful farming operations of their own, so could not help their father and also continue to maintain their own farming operations. Farming required many hours of hand labor to put in, cultivate and harvest the crops. They also had a variety of animals which required many hours to feed and provide care.

Andrew, the youngest son, was a rather nice-looking man in his early to mid-thirties. He had a pleasant smile like his mother and was warm and welcoming to the young couple. Jacob, the older of the two, bigger than his brother, and unlike Andrew's friendliness, Jacob had a menacing appearance. He had two front teeth missing, ten days growth of beard, long rather unkept hair and a facial expression that exuded hostility.

Everyone sat around the table to wait for Jenny, Andrew's wife, to arrive. Meanwhile Nina put the finishing touches on the meal. Martha was anxious to meet Jenny since both women were about the same age. She was looking forward to finding companionship in another woman. She missed her friends back in Mobridge. Jenny did not disappoint when she arrived. She had a warm and welcoming smile for Martha and eagerly shared information about life in this new world.

After dinner the men went to talk about work and Nina and Jenny visited with Martha. Since it was getting late and the newcomers needed to get settled into their new home, conversation ended with Jenny and Nina escorting Martha and Martin to their new quarters which was a cabin about ten feet by twelve feet. It was modestly furnished with a bed, table and two chairs, a chest of drawers for clothes and a rocking chair. The cooking stove was old but serviceable and the shelves above it would hold dishes and a few pans. The fireplace was sturdy and would provide plenty of heat for the cold winters. The walls were built of thick unhued timber with a small window carved for light.

Over the next weeks, Martha found Jenny to be a trusted friend as their many conversations became more relaxed and enjoyable. These two young women were developing a close relationship that would bloom and support them both over the next five decades.

Martha knew that Jacob had a twelve-year old son. She asked Jenny, "Where is the boy's mother?" The smile left Jenny's face and was followed by a long pause where no one spoke. The gravity of the conversation had clearly changed. Jenny could see the determination in Martha's question and replied that Jacob's wife, Anne, had died less than one week ago from what many believe was a drunken rage on Jacob's part. Jacob claimed that Anne had fallen into a pen with a bull and was killed by the attacking animal. Jacob had claimed that the attack had come with such speed that he could not reach his wife in time to save her.

Jenny told Martha that most everyone in the community doubted his explanation. She said that neither she nor Andrew thought that the bull had killed Anne, but had to accept his explanation since there was no opportunity to find out what had really happened.

After another pause, Jenny said, "We believe that she died as a result of one of Jacob's intoxicated rages."

Over the years, Jenny and others had seen Anne with a bruised face and bandages over various parts of her body. She always had an explanation for her bruised appearance and never accused Jacob of beating her. Jacob always denied hitting her. After one such episode, she had to walk with a cane for nearly a year. It was so sad because had she said something, perhaps Andrew and his father might have been able to intervene. They both sat in a mournful sadness trying to understand how a person could be born with such an evil heart.

They both knew that situations like this were uncommon but still happening with alarming frequency. Martha thanked Jenny for the information and mournfully excused herself from the parlor and her half-filled cup of tea. She went home to think about Anne and her sad demise.

Days passed as the Canadian cold set in during late November and early December. They awoke one morning in mid-December to a ten-inch snowfall and a temperature in single digits. Martin said he would get Emil and they would hitch the horses to the wagon to go to town for needed supplies. Since the distance was over five miles, they would not return until sometime after dark because it would be difficult for the horses and wagon to cut through the heavy snow.

While Martin was gone to town with Emil, Martha began boiling water for washing clothes. When she was finished with the washing, she would hang them in the small room to dry. She was also preparing a mix of cornmeal with a small lamb hock for Martin's evening meal. She knew that he would be cold and hungry when he returned home. Midway through the meal preparation, with her back to the heavy door, she heard the door rub against its tight frame. Startled by the sound, she quickly turned and faced the door.

There stood Jacob. He was intoxicated. He had a wide grin

that exposed his many missing teeth. The ten-day growth of beard, dirty clothes and squinting eyes greeted Martha's first look. He stood in the doorway continuing his smile and said nothing. No more than six feet separated them. Terrified, but gaining in strength, she offered Jacob a cup of tea. She turned with her back to Jacob feigning an effort to pour the hot tea while she slowly slipped her hand into a drawer near the ancient stove. She felt for the handle of the Colt forty-five revolver. She gripped the handle, freed it from the drawer and turned to face Jacob.

He continued to smile, seemingly disregarding the heavy gun. He began to take a step forward as he said, "I want you, Missy. You come to me. You are very pretty and I like pretty women."

Martha's brain raced through the options that she had in this most dangerous situation. She had never imagined anything like this, but she was well aware that she had the upper hand. Jacob did not seem to be convinced that he was also in peril as Martha squared to face him. The consequences of this situation seemed endless and Martha's first behavior would determine the outcome. It did not seem as if anything good could come from this.

The barrel of the gun was focused forty inches from Jacob's belly. Martha felt her finger begin to tighten on the cold trigger. As Jacob reached to grab her, the room exploded with sound and then fell silent. Jacob finally uttered a groan and froze with his eyes never leaving Martha's face. As he fell to the floor with streams of blood and body fluids coming from his front and back, his eyes remained open. It was as if the empty stare was consuming all of the universe at once.

As Martha viewed the Jacob's face, she now felt the horror of the situation. Thoughts raced around in her head and really made no sense. As Jacob lay on the floor staring into space, pools of blood and fluid began to form a large circle around his body. It nearly filled the small room.

Martha stood in silence. It seemed like an eternity. She slowly moved toward the door but simply could not avoid stepping in some blood because the room was small. She knew that she had to look for someone to tell, but who. As she stepped outside in a frightened panic with no wrap, she was met by the stiffening cold. Martin was gone, so her thoughts immediately went to Jenny. After all, it was Jenny who let her know that Jacob was dangerous and to be very careful around him.

Martha felt an intense anxiety with no regret. This had to be done and she was strong enough to do it.

She opened Jenny's door without a knock. The shock and panic on her face let Jenny know that something had happened, and it was serious. Martha still held the Colt forty-five in her shaking hand. A surprised look fell over Jenny's face at the sight of the weapon.

Standing in the doorway shaking, Martha blurted, "I shot him."

Jenny immediately knew who the victim was. She then moved to embrace her new friend. Both wept for what seemed like a long time without exchanging words. Jenny felt no remorse for the dead man, but instead began to fear for Martha's future. Jenny had never heard of a woman taking a man's life in an effort to protect herself.

Would the Royal Canadian Mounted Police and the local magistrates have any sympathy for a woman who shot a man? Would they charge her with murder? With an exchange of facial expressions and with resignation they knew that the authorities must be notified. The Mounted Police would do the investigation. They were located almost eighty miles away in the city of Edmonton. Jacob's lifeless body could not be moved until someone with authority arrived.

Martha refused to return to the tiny home covered with blood. Hours later Martin and Emil returned to be confronted by two scared and sobbing women. They stood still and asked no questions of the distraught women. With the agony of a father, Emil knew how this event came to be. He, too, had suspected that Jacob had killed Anne in a fit of rage. He knew that Jacob was a dangerous man. He worried about telling his wife, Nina, about the death of their oldest son at the hands of this young woman whom they had welcomed into their family.

Martin could not believe that this very young and timid German girl had turned into a woman of confidence who understood when she needed to protect herself. She had just killed someone who was attempting to rape her.

After telling a grieving Nina about Jacob, Emil took the horses and wagon back to town, so a constable could be notified of the situation. Their small town had no law enforcement personnel, so a constable would have to come from a larger community over twenty miles away.

Martin and Martha stayed with Jenny because they couldn't bear to go back to their home with Jacob's body lying on the floor. The next day, a constable arrived late in the afternoon. He took charge of the situation and had the body moved to a cold room for preservation while waiting for the mounted police to arrive from Edmonton. `

Jenny and Martha scrubbed the floor until all traces of blood were erased. Somehow their small home looked frightening and hostile. Martha could not bear to be in it alone, so the young couple stayed with Jenny waiting for the mounted police to arrive.

Three days later the mounted police representative rode into the yard to investigate the crime and gather information to be presented to the magistrate committee in Edmonton. The gentleman was polite and respectful of all the people as he asked questions and gathered information. He would take what he learned to Edmonton for a review with a three-magistrate committee. The magistrate committee would decide what was to be done with Martha as a result of her action.

The days passed slowly for the young couple as they waited for instructions as to how they should proceed. Nina had accepted Martha's story because she had suspected that Jacob had abused Anne. She also confided in Jenny that she believed that Jacob had killed Anne but she hated to believe that her son could do such a terrible thing. Still Jacob was her son and she grieved his loss. She had prayed so many times that he would change, but he only seemed to get worse as he grew older.

Three weeks had passed before Martha received a directive from the magistrate court to appear and make a plea on her case. Again, Martha had to face an eighty-mile journey in an old wagon to the city of Edmonton. People in Lakeview had no idea what the court's reaction to Martha's action might be. Local thought ranged from execution for cold-blooded murder to the release of a woman who was simply defending herself against a potential rapist.

This time she did not notice the bouncing wagon with no cushion. Her thoughts were dominated by having to meet with people of authority that she had never seen before and whose ideas she had never heard before. Arriving in Edmonton, they looked for the magistrate building where the Canadian review would be held. They hoped that all the facts would be considered. A man was dead. He was killed by a young woman and the only living witness was the woman herself. Information was given to the magistrate by the investigating officers for the court's consideration.

Martin and Martha entered the courtroom with the high ceiling. They looked up to a bench where three white men sat wearing black robes. These men were expressionless but maintained intense eye contact with Martha. Martin's face reflected his fears while Martha's look was straight ahead and without emotion.

Jenny and her husband, Andrew, came with Martin and Martha to lend support to this young couple. Jenny asked to speak to the magistrates.

She said, "I believe that the decedent was attempting to take advantage of Martha, and she was in grave danger. I also believe that there is a high likelihood that this man killed his wife and blamed it on an attack by a raging bull. I also know that he regularly hit his son and was feared by many in the community."

In their years, the magistrates had not heard of a woman so aggressively defending herself from a violent man. This troubled and amazed them. The testimonials were short. The magistrates showed no emotion as they entered their chambers for discussion. Their discussions in chambers reflected that they did not want to show sympathy for anyone who had taken another person's life, particularly this young German woman who spoke in broken English. They had to find some way to punish her while at the same time recognizing that she may have had no other choice.

The few people in the room sat quietly for what seemed like hours. The side door finally opened and the three men entered with no smiles never looking at Martha. The man in the center called the room to order and stated the directives. Martha's face remained firm as she listened to their verdict.

"Martha Schreader, you are hereby sentenced to two years in the province jail. Due to the mitigating circumstances of this disaster, you are being offered the option of leaving this nation within six weeks. This court will pay the expenses of a train ticket from Calgary to the city of Winnipeg and on to Fargo, North Dakota, in the United States. If you choose this option, and we hope you will, you must never return to the Commonwealth of Canada. If you do return, you will be arrested immediately."

The wagon ride from the meeting with the magistrates was filled with a full range of feelings from optimism to another loss. Once again, Martha was required to give up someone who had become trusted and dear to her heart. She had come to trust and enjoy Jenny's company. The two women had grown close in a short time.

Although Martin had mixed feelings about losing his new employer, Emil, he realized that Martha had just escaped a serious interaction with the law. In a strange sort of way, Martha felt the guilt of killing another person yet, simultaneously, the relief that accompanied an escape from paying for it with her freedom.

Once again, her life would have to begin anew. For the Schreader couple, the idea of living in the United States had seemed so simple in Germany, but had turned into a desperate seemingly constant search for a place to find this life.

As the wagon bumped on, Martin placed his arm over Martha's shoulder feeling a sense of guilt. He had not been part of something that touched Martha's life so harshly. He had not been there to protect her. He had not tried to speak to Jacob telling him that he should never enter his home. Perhaps he had been too kind toward the man in an effort to extend the hand of friendship. He wondered if things could have been better somehow if they had chosen to immigrate to South America instead of to the United States.

Upon returning to Lakeview which later was changed to Provost, Martha asked if she could stay with Jenny and not return to the small cabin that she had once called her home. She did not want to view the irregular pattern of the blood-stained floor.

Those memories were returning during the long winter nights in the form of a cold sweat and that had terrified her. Those nightmares would persist for many years.

CHAPTER 16

NEW RESPONSIBILITIES

IN THE FIRST HOURS OF MARTHA'S ARRIVAL in Jenny and Andrew's small home, she heard a tiny squeak come from a box in the corner of the room. Others in the room also heard the sound. With caution, Jenny went to the box as if she had been caught in some type of guilty endeavor. The sound came again while Jenny reached over and picked up a small flannel blanket with something inside. It was a tiny baby. Jenny held the child in the blanket and gazed around the room. The faces she surveyed registered surprise and confusion. Jenny was cautious as she began to think about how she would explain the presence of this tiny baby girl.

Jenny explained that this child had been born to Anne just before she was killed. Jacob took no responsibility for the infant's life. However, this little child named Emma had a big brother by the name of David. He was twelve years old. People noted that this boy frequently appeared with eyes swollen shut and various bruises over his body. Without really observing what had occurred, everyone knew that the boy's assailant was his drunken father, Jacob.

Martha and Martin had never seen David as he had shuttered himself in a small room next to the barn. He seldom dared to show his face. While living in the barn, David had learned to care for the few animals housed in the small pens.

He had often slept with them. They provided warmth to him during cold nights. He became skilled in the area of animal husbandry. He frequently took care of small goats that were abandoned by their mother. He learned to gather nourishment from the sheep and goats for the abandoned creatures. He fed them with his little finger that he placed in fresh milk and then laid the liquid on the lips of the infant animals. Most survived from his care.

As the years passed he became more efficient in nursing these helpless creatures making small tubes that released warm milk into their mouths. After his mother died from her wounds shortly after Emma's birth, David took over the responsibility of finding nourishment for this infant child, his sister.

For over a three-month period he had kept this child alive. The nourishment was poor. Emma grew very little and was tiny for an infant of three months. She was weak and vulnerable to disease. Jenny did not attempt to intervene while Jacob was alive. She feared for her own safety.

Immediately after Jacob's death, Jenny found David. He hardly knew who she was since he ventured out from the barn so seldom. She coaxed David into her care and brought the baby into the house. Every day there seemed to be a battle to keep this child alive. Jenny now had to care for a frightened boy and a desperate infant.

Martin and Martha looked upon this situation with a mixture of horror and anxiety. Martha had already had the experience of looking at a tiny developed infant that had died. She could not imagine that experience again in such a short period of time. Her mind raced. With racing thoughts, she had an idea. Would it be possible for her to become a surrogate mother to this child? Thoughts raced as she wondered whether her breasts still might contain some milk. Without words she sat in the small room and opened her blouse revealing her front.

She said, "Give me Emma."

Jenny, holding the baby, gently offered her to the seated Martha. Martha took the child softly, opened the blanket, and touched the child's lips to her nipple. At first there was nothing. After what seemed to be an eternity, the infant's lips began to search for nourishment.

After days of receiving of tiny amounts of nourishment, it became apparent that the infant's likelihood of survival was growing. It was also clear that Martha could not be separated from this baby.

Martin and Andrew again got into the wagon and made their way to Edmonton. They planned to ask the magistrate for more time for Martha to remain in the country. They explained that the tiny infant needed a wet-nurse to ensure its life. The only person that could provide that nourishment had been ordered to leave the country within days.

Their request was immediately denied.

Martin and Andrew made their way back to the village with the news. Those in the little house sunk into despair. Emma's survival seemed doomed without Martha. However, Jenny and Martha were determined not to let this happen, so they decided that the baby would have to travel with Martha for the thirteen hundred miles to Fargo, North Dakota.

This new solution presented additional stress and anxiety for the two women. Jenny was sad because she would be separated not only from Martha but also from Emma. Martha was feeling the weight of her imminent separation from Jenny but also the impending responsibility of caring for a tiny infant.

This this new turn of events was difficult for twelve-year old David to comprehend. His language skills were limited and his knowledge beyond the village was almost nonexistent. After hours of anxiety, David insisted that he travel with the infant he had nourished and grown to love. He seemed able to understand that that he must go with Martin and Martha away from the only life he had ever known. He cried when facing this uncertain future but was determined to go with them.

Plans had to be quickly made to get to Calgary, nearly one hundred and twenty miles from their current location. There they would find relief from the cold and harsh winds. Martha needed protection and warmth to protect her while she was providing nurturance to this fragile baby.

Again the family was traveling, but now there were four. A young man and woman with a primitive boy and a little baby girl who flirted with death. They had to learn to take care of each other.

The trip to Calgary was to take four days with no promise of a train that would be ready to travel to the East. The little wagon was uncomfortable and bumpy as it bounced over the frozen dirt. For the first time the baby cried rather than squeaked. David sat almost motionless without words responding only to direct instructions. He was frightened. Each day required efforts to find small places for rent so that the family could warm themselves. One night this task was not possible, and they were forced to sleep under the stars. They huddled tightly together to preserve their warmth and to keep Emma from perishing from the cold.

Upon arriving in Calgary, they went immediately to the Catholic Church rectory. There they were able to find food and gather information as to train connections. There would be a train leaving the station the following day for Winnipeg. Martin gave the horse and wagon to the priest as a thank you for the respite from the extreme weather while they waited for the train connections.

Meanwhile, Emma continued to show signs of improving health. The train ride to Winnipeg would take approximately two days. All of the money the young couple possessed had been used to buy the tickets from Calgary to Winnipeg.

Once arriving in Winnipeg, there was no money left for the shorter ride from Winnipeg to Fargo, North Dakota. The priest from the Catholic Church in Calgary had given the family a letter of introduction to the priest in the Catholic Church in Winnipeg. He had sent a request for the Winnipeg parish to provide charitable funds to enable the young family to purchase passage on a train traveling south to Fargo. To their relief, the priest in Winnipeg was able to secure tickets on the train headed for Fargo.

The five days of travel were uneventful with the baby crying slightly louder and David gazing out the window saying nothing. Martha busied herself with caring for Emma and David. Martin worried about what challenges they would face in Fargo as he clasped yet another letter of introduction from the priest in Winnipeg.

After arriving in Fargo, the family quickly made their way to the Catholic Church. They presented the priest, Father Lindstrom, with their newest letter of introduction. He recommended that the young couple with the sick baby and the withdrawn boy immediately move into the rectory. Winter weather in January, posed a life-threatening situation for such a fragile infant.

At long last, in the safety and warmth of the rectory, Martha had time to reflect. Emma was easy to love. She bonded with Martha and captured the soul of Martin. She would become God's gift of love in the absence of Elizabeth. Holding Emma tightly on the softer chairs in the rectory, Martha thought of how much she would like to show this child to Edith back in Bristol.

She caught herself thinking that she had nearly forgotten the two women from the saloon. It was their counsel and concern that set the direction for this wonderful happening. They had modeled the behavior that enabled Martha to stand tall in the face of an attack. They had taught her to shoot and encouraged her to be strong.

The tiny baby seemed to take soft and gentle naps now. The fussing had nearly stopped. As Emma began to thrive, Martha started thinking about the young boy, David. He was the one who had really saved little Emma's life. He had kept her alive during those first difficult days after their mother's death. It was his gentleness and love caring for Emma that enabled her to live long enough for Martha to be able to step in and provide the nourishment needed for survival. She wondered if he had any real possibilities for a good life.

He still remained distant with a vocabulary that contained only a few English words. By this time, Martha could understand nearly all of them. Father Lindstrom knew that the quiet, withdrawn boy was cause for concern. In order to understand his capabilities and to draw him out from his shell, Father assigned him many tasks at the rectory and the church. Each task offered more complexity than the previous one. Interestingly, he noted that the boy opened himself to problem-solving in areas from cleaning to carpentry. One day while building a bookcase for the rectory, David asked Father Lindstrom to tell him about words. This was a rather surprising request from a child of this age.

Father Lindstrom also watched Martin work at the church and participate in religious ceremonies. He began to feel an attachment to this man's future. While drinking tea one evening, he suggested to Martin that he might consider working for Father Lindstrom's family who owned a shipping company in the harbor of Duluth, Minnesota. He explained that help was needed and that wages were very good. Martin understood farm crops but really had no idea how they were managed in large quantities of grain around a shipping port.

However, after thinking about what Father Lindstrom said, he truly saw an opportunity to support Martha and the two young children that were now his responsibility. Martin also recognized that for the first time he had entered a non-frontier area. He had never lived in one. Even in Germany, their village was small and isolated. He remembered passing through Minneapolis, Minnesota, on their travels west to Mobridge, South Dakota, and he thought about the many buildings and people busily walking about the streets. There were boarded sidewalks instead of dirt, oil lamps on each corner and businesses along the way.

With the recommendation of Father Lindstrom in hand, Martin decided to leave for Duluth. He would have Martha stay in the rectory until he had a place for his new, young family to live. Father Lindstrom gave strong support to the idea. The priest advanced Martin the money he would need to get to Duluth and find a place to stay while looking for housing and a job at the docks. One of the recommendations he had given Martin was a letter of introduction to his family.

The next day, Martin set off for Duluth. When he arrived, the Lindstrom family welcomed him with open arms and advanced him additional money to enable him to begin his search for housing for himself and his family. They were confident that their son, the priest, was a very good judge of a man's character, so they did not hesitate to give Martin a job with good wages. They very quickly recognized that Martin was a good worker and were very pleased with their decision to hire him.

CHAPTER 17

TIME TO LEARN AND GROW

OVER THE NEXT MONTHS, Father Lindstrom spent time with David teaching him letters and words. David seemed to understand many concepts even though they were never part of his previous life. The boy attached strongly to the priest. Father Lindstrom realized that this boy was intelligent but very far behind in his schooling. He discussed an idea with Martha that included sending David to a school in Onamia, Minnesota, where young boys of about David's age were beginning their training for the priesthood. The education included many things beyond religious study. After considerable thought, Martha came to realize that this education would be a good opportunity for David. She could see how quickly David learned everything the priest was teaching him.

Father Lindstrom had been planning a trip to Onamia when the weather warmed for himself to renew his friendships with his fellow priests. He asked Martha if David could go with him. Again, Martha agreed to allow the priest to discuss this idea with David.

The trip to Onamia with Father Lindstrom would be up to David. She would allow him to make that decision. Once David agreed to travel to Onamia with Father Lindstrom, they began to engage in lengthy discussions about beginning the long and complex education that David would undertake if he decided to stay in Onamia. With each discussion smiles grew broader and David became more excited every day about the possibility of learning in such an esteemed place.

Martha agreed to tend to the church rectory while Father Lindstrom and David began the nearly two-hundred-mile journey to Onamia, Minnesota. Father Lindstrom clearly felt that David should stay at the Catholic boarding school to begin his academic studies. David also seemed eager to embrace this education which Father Lindstrom had been explaining.

Despite their enthusiasm for this new possibility, the priest worried that the clergy in charge of the school at Onamia might not accept David. He was far behind the other boys who were studying to become priests. The environment there was strange. The boys were required to begin their day at five in the morning for daily mass. After that they would eat a simple breakfast and begin their studies. They were required to work at the seminary before dinner and study for several hours each night before bed.

Since David had not yet been baptized, the overseers of the school would engage in the baptismal ritual if and when they believed that David could manage the rigorous studies. The young boys sang religious songs at daily mass.

David sat quietly only observing the strange uniform behavior in the room. He was dressed in old clothes from donations to the Fargo church. His presence attracted attention and puzzlement from the other boys who were now well into the ritual studies. David was no stranger to fear but felt clumsy and disoriented in this environment. He cried. He knew of no feelings other than survival in his past life. He could not sleep; however, he did feel some sense of physical safety.

After two weeks, it was necessary for Father Lindstrom to leave. The possibility of being without this nurturing priest struck terror in the boy. After two nights of highly emotional and ambivalent discussion, David and Father Lindstrom agreed that David would stay. Father Lindstrom would write frequently and David would simply learn to write with the help of an older boy. This new world was filled with uncertainty and anticipation. However frightened David was in this unfamiliar place, he felt determined to succeed.

CHAPTER 18

DULUTH'S CHALLENGES

For Martin the work at the port was hard. Possibilities for a good life seemed to now gain some shape in his mind. There was change in the air. Martin was able to save money. Martha felt that in a matter of weeks, she would travel to Duluth to join Martin who had sent letters of encouragement about his new job. The little baby was beginning to find her health. She was eating some solid food and drinking milk from the market. She was a friendly child who embraced her surrogate mother, Martha, with warmth and kisses.

Martha and Emma made the trip from Fargo to Duluth with ease. Emma slept in Martha's arms and found time to make fingerprints on the steamed passenger car window of the train. The one room apartment near the waterfront had a full stock of food from the very first evening of their arrival. Martin had cleaned the room to perfection as he waited for his beloved wife and their new child to arrive. It seemed as if nothing could go wrong and their life was finally headed in the direction that both had dreamed about when they left Germany.

As the months passed, little Emma was speaking a mixture of English and German. She was now beginning to talk. She seemed to love trying to say words. Martha was busy caring for their small apartment and taking care of Emma who continued to grow and thrive. Martin was succeeding at his job and enjoyed the challenges the hard work presented him.

Since Martin was a responsible man at the harbor, he was quickly given the job of managing the shoots that filled the ships. This was dangerous work. It would be easy to slip and fall into the hold of the ship that the shoot was filling with grain. It had happened before, killing the victim in every instance.

One day following an ice storm, Martin fell. He screamed and thrashed attempting to keep himself above the flowing grain. His body disappeared. One of his fellow workers who was also slipping on the ice noticed that Martin was no longer there. He was sure he knew what had happened but had no idea how long Martin had been buried.

He quickly stopped the loading shoot and grabbed the edge of the ship's hold. He screamed into the partially filled hold, but there was no sound. He screamed for help. Others knowing the immense danger of this work quickly arrived at the scene of the accident. They immediately began lowering themselves into the hold of the ship listening for sound and looking for movement. After what seemed like hours, one of the workers noticed a slight movement in the grain. They rapidly began to dig, shouting encouragement to each other, trying to save Martin's life. These shipyard workers had formed a brotherhood. They would all risk their own lives to save another.

A co-worker strained his reach for Martin's slightly exposed wrist. He clung tightly to the rope with one hand and pulled Martin's limp body from the shifting grain with the other. Additional men ran down with ropes and fastened a halter around Martin's chest. No one knew if he was dead or alive.

Once they had Martin out of the ship's hold, they laid him on the deck of the guardhouse. They shouted his name and pushed on his chest. His chest heaved as he began coughing. His lungs had become clogged with grain dust as Martin held his breath trying to prevent breathing in the deadly grain. He weakly began to breathe. In his confusion he struggled and tossed, hitting his head, arms and legs against the hard floor. The shipyard workers immediately held his body to the floor as the coughing grew more violent.

Martha could not understand why her husband was so late in coming home from work. She began to fret and worry about what had delayed him. Eventually his fellow workers lifted him onto a cart and pulled it to the small apartment. Martha ran to the cart and hugged Martin asking the men what had happened to him. They told her as she clung to Martin in tears. Martin was unable to recognize Martha because he was so disoriented from the trauma that he had endured. They quickly lifted Martin into the small apartment where they were able to make him comfortable in his bed. As the days passed, it became apparent that Martin would make some recovery from his ordeal. He continued to cough with small particles of grain flying periodically from his lungs. Martha took great care of him trying to nurse him back to health. His foreman had insisted that he stay home with Martha and Emma until he felt recovered enough to work.

Martin pushed himself to recover because the small family needed the money that his job gave them. They could not go long without Martin's paycheck. Days passed with Martha begging Martin to never again go on the deck of the ship to work the grain shoot.

Within his heart he knew he had to beg his boss to find him other work on the docks. He worried that he might be fired. The foreman, a kind man, offered him another job with equal pay. He knew Martin was a hard worker and did not want to lose him. He asked Martin if he would consider becoming a purchaser of grains in west central Minnesota.

Such a job would require Martin to be gone from home for extended periods of time. This caused him great concern because he would have to leave Martha and Emma in Duluth. Martha assured him that she would be safe among the new friends that she made at the rooming house. She still kept her Colt forty-five handy.

Martin accepted the new job once he felt well enough to travel. Martha prepared a bag of clothing for Martin's travels. He would be riding by train in a red railcar at the back end of the long line of cars. He was also told that he would now meet with grain stations in the communities of Morris, Chokio, and Alberta. These were names of places that he had never heard of before. The new adventure was beginning.

CHAPTER 19

MARTIN'S NEW JOB

MARTIN'S RESPONSIBLE CHARACTER AND INTELLIGENCE and his understanding of agricultural grains made him an ideal fit for this new challenge. He was able to connect with the local grain handlers and arranged for orderly shipments of materials to the great harbor in Duluth. The grain needed to be provided in a timely manner. Too much grain made storage impossible. Too little grain meant that ships had to wait for products to arrive. Making sure that everything ran smoothly was difficult but Martin was able to handle this new assignment with ease. He had a natural knack for estimating the amount of gain that would be needed for each shipment.

After each shipment was arranged, Martin was able to travel back home to Duluth. He accompanied the grain on the train hauling it to the port. This enabled him to live with his family until the train was emptied and sent back to west central Minnesota. Each departure was accompanied with sadness and tears from both Martin and Martha. They hated being apart for so much of the time. Yet the money was good and their savings was beginning to grow.

After a year, Martin was beginning to tire of the work and desperately wanted to make arrangements for his family to be together. By this time, he knew some farmers in the area who told him of a small farm that was for sale. He had saved enough money to make a down payment on a small acreage near Alberta, Minnesota. The home on the property was weather-beaten and without heat but appeared fixable. He was excited with the prospect of his family being together on their own farm. Finally, his dream of a new life might be happening.

Martin had met a nearby farm family by the name of Eystad. A father and mother with eight little boys. The friendship matured rapidly. During their free time, the Eystad family of Alberta helped Martin work to make the house livable for himself and his family. With many hands from the two men and eight strong boys, the house was made livable.

The move from Duluth to Alberta was simple. Emma and Martha traveled in the small red railcar behind a long line of railcars pulled by a large steam engine. The car was warm and comfortable. Martha made conversation with a man who wore a police style cap and seemed to be in charge. Emma played with another little girl who was also traveling with her mother. Martha was excited to see the farm because Martin had told her so much about their new home and the wonderful neighbors who had helped them prepare the house.

Martin was waiting at the train station with his newly purchased horse drawn wagon. They embraced and began their new life with excitement and enthusiasm.

The small farm would not produce any revenue during the first year, so Martin searched for work in town. He contacted an acquaintance, Francis Gieselman who agreed to hire him for his maintenance shop in Alberta. Francis knew that Martin was very clever with his hands and would be able to help him keep up with all the work.

The stage seemed to be set for settling down.

The family was very happy with their new life together in Alberta. Martin worked full-time on his farm, but also helped Francis when the work load became too much for him. Martha was busy keeping the house and teaching Emma skills in gardening, baking and sewing.

Emma was now six years old so Martha took her to school for the first time. She attended a one-room school with eleven children. Emma was the youngest. That year Martha became pregnant and delivered a small boy baptized with the name of Aloysius.

No one questioned Emma's presence or wondered about her lineage. She was just another kid in a small village that had many children. Two more babies followed, so now there were four children. The small house was becoming crowded. Soon they would need to build an addition. Martin and Martha spent hours talking about how they would create this addition to their home.

CHAPTER 20

A NEW CHALLENGE

MEANWHILE, THIS FAMILY AND THE WHOLE COUNTRY would soon be facing a new challenge. The year was 1918 and rumors were spreading about a disease that was killing small children and adults by the thousands. That year in Fort Riley, Kansas, several soldiers became sick as they were preparing to leave for World War I. The disease spread rapidly throughout the camp and eventually throughout the world as soldiers were being sent to France and other parts of the globe. The H1N1 flu virus infected one third of the Earth's population, five hundred million people. Between twenty million and fifty million people worldwide would die. There was no place to hide from this horrible disease.

Emma and her little brother, Al became infected with the flu. Al's case was slight, and he was able to quickly recover, but Emma became very sick with her temperature rising to nearly fatal degrees. Her cough was shallow with little strength. She simply laid on her small bed or in Martha's arms gazing at the face of the only mother that she had ever known. There were times that Martha thought that this child had lost her will to survive. She could not imagine being separated from someone she had grown to so passionately love.

Emma's survival was in doubt. Martha and Martin prayed

fervently for Emma to recover. With what seemed like a miracle, the weakened child began to slowing gain strength.

Shortly after Emma recovered and had gained her strength back, a letter arrived for Martha. It was from Jenny. Jenny had decided to move her family from Provost, Canada, to Rochester, Minnesota. Her husband, Andrew, had died from the flu along with his mother. This left her alone with her elderly father-in-law, Emil. She already knew that her niece, Emma, was vulnerable to poor health and that Emil was getting very old and weak.

Jenny disposed of all the family property in north central Canada and prepared to move to a town where she had heard there was a facility that could provide excellent healthcare. She felt this was important for Emil and for Emma's long-term survival.

This letter from Jenny was a crushing blow to Martha. She loved Emma more than life itself. She always knew that Jenny would someday return to care for this beautiful child, but Martha had never allowed herself to think about this day. She had a firm agreement with Jenny that she would never stand in the way if such a time occurred.

She put the letter down and cried. Emma said, "Mama, why are you crying?"

Martha did not want to frighten the child, so she said, "Emma, these are tears of joy because your aunt Jenny is returning to us and will be a part of our lives."

Secretly, she hoped Jenny would change her mind.

Jenny did not change her mind and arrived with Emil several months later. She and Emil rode the train to Morris where Martin, Martha and Emma met them. The meeting was bittersweet. Martha was filled with sadness with the thought that a child she had raised for over a decade and nurtured to life many times would now be gone.

A New Challenge

Jenny was anxious and nervous at the thought that she was now thrusting herself into Emma's life. She was a total stranger to Emma and worried that Emma would reject her. Cautious hugs were exchanged between the women, and Emil shook Martin's hand. Emma stood with a confused expression on her face as she observed the scene.

Jenny bent over Emma not asking her for a hug but, instead, trying to understand the expression on the child's face. Emma seemed to know that this new person was going to be a very important part of her life. The child's face reflected an interest in Jenny as she clung to Martha's hand.

Martha said, "How long will you be able to stay in our home?"

Jenny responded, "I have no reason to hurry. Perhaps you would like to travel with me to Rochester while I find a home suitable for Emma, Emil and me."

Martha's face lit with excitement. She had only been away from Alberta for a few days over the past six years. The bond of cooperation and mutual respect was beginning to build again between the two friends.

If Martha was to travel to Rochester with Jenny, one of her friends would simply have to come to the house to help with the children while Martin was in the field. Emma at ten was too young to be left with that responsibility by herself.

CHAPTER 21

FOUNDATION FOR AN EVENT

THE NEXT 20 YEARS WERE FILLED WITH EXCITEMENT and success for this Alberta, Minnesota, family. Martin Schreader had become a successful farmer and a respected mechanic in central Minnesota. Martin continued to be an easy-going hard-working German immigrant who spoke with an accent that was easily recognized by his new friends and neighbors.

Friends and neighbors trusted Martin and brought their business to him. Martha, on the other hand, was still an attractive young German woman even though she had become less trusting and more self- reliant. She still kept her Colt forty-five handy, not even Martin knew it was nearby.

Martin's oldest son, Al, became a popular businessman in the area of machine repair. He was very much attracted to automobiles and hoped that one day he could sell them to the residents of Traverse and Grant Counties. Even though he could not afford one for himself, he always took good care of his customers who brought their automobiles to him for repair.

Al and his father, who were described as friendly and easy-going men, frequently made deals that Martha found unsatisfactory. The neighborhood knew of her as a woman who would not easily accept compromise and had a more rigid approach to life and to business.

One day Martin decided to sell thirty-seven ton of cast-iron to a smelting plant in Gary, Indiana. The delivered purchase price was eighteen dollars per ton. The agreement said that the seller had the option of delivering the cast-iron over the next twelve months. Since there was no stated date for delivery, the price could fluctuate depending upon existing markets.

Martha tried to convince Martin that this was not a good business deal. Unfortunately, he ignored her advice and before all the materials were delivered that year, the price had risen to thirty-two dollars per ton. The smelting company indicated that they would not compensate for any price change. They would only pay the prior agreed eighteen dollars for the final delivery.

Martin reluctantly agreed with the buyer as Martha observed. She was upset with Martin that he didn't haggle with the buyer and insist that the current rate be paid for the cast-iron. She decided to take it upon herself to get the increased rate, so she wrote to the casting company in Gary, Indiana. She stated in her letter that she would come personally to their headquarters with legal action should they not pay the current market price of thirty-two dollars per ton.

The company felt no pressure from a little woman who spoke English with a German accent. Martha angrily boarded a train headed for Chicago, and with all the rage she could muster, she argued forcefully with the company management.

Somehow, her presence did not seem appropriate to those in the room but she did get attention. Threats and angry exchanges followed. The male managers were confused by the forcefulness of this determined lady. As time passed that day, the management caved to this fierce little lady and paid the full amount for the iron.

From then on, Martha became a force in the transactions carried out by her family.

Young Al had seen his father claim the riches of the 1920s and withstand the desperate days of the 1930s. They were learning how to do business in a rapidly changing economy. During these days, Al began to date a young woman, Myrtle Gieselman, who worked at the Penny's store in Morris. Their marriage was planned for the summer of 1939.

The couple was well known in the community. Everyone expected a large and enjoyable wedding ceremony at Assumption Catholic Church in Morris.

Jenny and Emma visited Martha each summer. The meetings were always warm and full of love. However, Emma was never given an explanation as to how these people came together in such an affectionate way.

The thought never crossed Emma's mind. She was a bright and determined young woman much like her surrogate mother, Martha, but with the warmth and love of her aunt Jenny. She had spent many days working at the famous Mayo Clinic in Rochester, Minnesota. People grew to love and respect Emma and encouraged her to become a physician.

With encouragement from her aunt and a few others, Emma enrolled in medical school at the University of Minnesota. The emotional stakes were high, there were few female physicians. Jenny knew that her niece would have a hard time gaining respect in an area that was so male-dominated.

Jenny frequently said to Emma, "Fight like a girl!" She wanted Emma to be herself but also to be strong and steadfast in her pursuit of her dream.

Emma did. She navigated the school with ease and became recognized as someone who could lead and practice medicine at the highest level.

With much fanfare, Emma's big brother, David, rejoined the family. He was now a priest and a wise leader. After much prayer, he reached a decision to practice his priestly duties at the clinic where his little sister was going to work.

He asked, "Aunt Jenny, I would like to live with you and my sister, Emma. I have almost no memory of a family, and today I would like to become part of one."

PART THREE

A COLLISION OF FAMILIES

CHAPTER 22

THE BEGINNING OF THE END

WHILE THE SCHREADER FAMILY CONTINUED TO GROW and prosper, the Hartman family struggled with Wayne's behavior issues. Ada had remarried after John's death. Morris Flint was a kind and gentle man who tried to help Ada with Wayne.

Wayne's life between the ages of seventeen and twenty-one was filled with chaos. He recklessly drove cars that he borrowed from well-meaning individuals. His work was occasional. He was known in the Elbow Lake area as a kid who was a loner and could not be trusted. He was always in need of money. On most occasions he was able to get it from his caring mother or his uncle, Ray Teft.

In late 1938, Ada decided that it would be good to try her dear son on a small farm. Her hope was that Wayne would begin to mature with this type of responsibility. Ada and Morris, her new husband, contacted the Haney Land Company in nearby Herman, Minnesota.

After some negotiation, they rented a small forty-acre farm for Wayne in the fall of 1938. He was given two draft horses and twenty-two pigs to begin his farming operation. Since the operation was new and the farm work was completed prior to their rental agreement, most of the buildings were empty. They were able to use a small building for the pig barn. To help warm the pigs, they used a fresh pile of straw that had been thrashed by the previous tenant.

Together they decided not to till the cropland for next year's harvest since Ada had purchased five hundred bushels of corn-on-the-cob to be used as animal feed over the winter. It was assumed that Wayne would live alone in the house and use an old 1928 Model A Ford for transportation.

The winter passed slowly, and Wayne stayed home alone most nights. The house was cold. It had only a small amount of furniture and no pictures. Wayne simply had no friends. To pass the time he would drive past the IOOF Hall in Norcross, Minnesota, on Friday and Saturday nights. This effort required him to drive the ten miles from his home to the town. Friends meant little to him. Only on rare occasions would he have a conversation with anyone. Since no one really seemed to know him, rumors were everywhere.

One Saturday evening when gas was running low in his car, he parked by the curb near front of the dance hall. There stood Sara Radke. Sara was a young woman of limited intelligence and without pretty clothes. Her family was poor since the Great Depression had left most people in poverty.

She was lonely and hoping for attention.

Wayne smiled and said, "Hello." He wanted to know where he could get gas for his car.

She told him, "We have a can of gas at my home. I can go with you to get it."

She was eager for attention and was pleased that this young, good looking man whom she had heard had money was talking to her. Most people just ignored her.

Wayne agreed and asked Sara to get into his car. She complied. They drove the short distance to her house in the old Model A. The Radke farm was about three miles from town.

The old house and run-down barn stood in a small grove of trees. They quickly located the gas can in the barn, and Wayne immediately poured the contents into his car. Afterwards, he noticed that Sara did not move toward the house.

"What do you want?" He asked.

She said, "I want to go back to town. I was inside the dance hall and only came out for a break from the smoke inside when you drove up."

"Ok. Climb inside the car, and we'll go back to town. By the way, thanks for the gas."

As the old car bumped along the three-mile drive back to the village there was no conversation. Wayne steered the car to the graveled Main Street and stopped in front of the dance hall.

On the front of the building was a clear block of cement with the inscription IOOF 1902. The building's presence was almost majestic since it was the largest building in the small village. There were no structures on either side of it.

Several years prior, much of Main Street was burned and several families died in the fire. As a result, all the buildings on either side of the dance hall were gone and there was no money to rebuild any of them. A small marker was set in a grassy area next to the building to commemorate the lost community members.

Tonight, the building was rocking with the loud music exploding from within. The band played for drinks and for fun. Everyone seemed to be having a good time. People were able to forget that they had been living with little hope or opportunity the past five years since this great depression had continued to linger.

Young men stood in front of the building smoking cigarettes and drinking Grain Belt Beer and talking to the young women who languished nearby. Most everyone had enough to drink to make anything someone said sound funny.

Once Wayne and Norma returned to the dance hall, she gave no indication that she wanted to go back inside.

Instead she said, "Can we go for a ride, so that I can see your house?"

She was thinking that Wayne could be a very good catch. She was told that Wayne's family had a considerable fortune.

He said, "Sure, why not."

He again started the old car, put it in gear and set the clutch.

The car chugged along the eight miles to Wayne's new farm. Since there was nothing else going on that interested him, he was willing to drive Sara to see his farm. This situation was puzzling to him because most of the young people in town ignored him. Here was this young woman who appeared interested in him. This was unfamiliar.

"Do you want some money for gas?" He asked her.

"Well my Dad will be pretty mad when he finds the gas can empty," replied Sara.

Wayne handed her fifty cents for the gas. She was thrilled since that was much more than the gas cost, which was proof that Wayne was wealthy.

The car's headlights outlined a structure hidden in the trees. It was a small home with attached rooms that were added as a family grew. This was a common practice for area Norwegian immigrants. German immigrants usually built large frame homes and expected to fill them with little ones as time passed. However, the more practical Norwegians build smaller homes and additional rooms as they were needed.

The old car made the house visible as the headlights focused. When Wayne shut off the engine, Sara quickly said, "Can we go inside?"

The Beginning of the End

Wayne agreed in his usual indifferent way.

They entered the small mudroom where the shoes were kept and overalls were hung since both usually smelled of the barnyard. Sara first noticed that the house was almost bare of furniture. On this mid-October evening the outside temperature was cooling. The house felt cold.

She said, noticing a woodpile, "I will get some wood and start a fire, it's cold in here."

In his usual manner, Wayne was indifferent. The new crackling fire warmed the home. As time passed, Sara gave no indication of wanting to go back to the dance.

She said, "It's getting late and I'm tired. Could I spend the night."

Again, Wayne had no response. He had not considered the request as either desirable or undesirable.

He responded, "OK."

Sara envisioned a romantic night with Wayne. Wayne, however, remained passively unresponsive to her overtures. In a rather awkward fashion Sara was able to achieve the response she desired from Wayne. Afterward, Wayne seemed uncertain as to what had just transpired. He certainly had no feelings for Sara and little interest in taking this encounter any further.

During the night the fire had gone out and the bedroom was cold. Sara loved being close to Wayne as they shared warmth. When the sun was fully up and lit the kitchen, she rose from the bed and fumbled around the kitchen looking for food. She treasured her experience of the last twelve hours. She knew that if she could inspire some interest on the part of Wayne, her days in poverty would be over.

She took up the Spartan challenge over the next month. Wayne eventually gave in to Sara's advances and agreed to marry her. The wedding was set for late December 1938. Ada was delighted to think that someone else seemed to know and love her son. Her husband, Morris, was not so sure. He was well aware of Wayne's unusual temperament and felt that this marriage could only end in disaster.

The cold winter of 1939 was filled with boredom for Wayne and his new wife, Sara. For recreation they visited Sara's family and made multiple trips to Elbow Lake to see his mother and stepfather. Uncle Raymond and his wife and new baby occasionally joined in for conversation when the young couple visited Elbow Lake.

On almost every trip, Wayne asked his mother for money. Since she was enjoying some wealth with her new husband, she frequently gave in to the young man. She hoped and prayed that this farming experience with the support of Sara would begin a new life. She wished that he could somehow forgo his troubled past.

Wayne continued to look for cars to drive with only occasional success. He kept twenty-five dollars in his pocket to offer as a down payment and to show that his interest was genuine. Most people knew his mother now had some money, so they were led to believe that Wayne could actually pay for the cars he asked to test drive.

During that winter he drove nineteen different automobiles. On a warm day in late March of 1939, he passed the Schreader gas station and car lot in Herman, Minnesota, on the way to visit his mother. That day Al Schreader had just received a shiny 1936 Chrysler. The car was delivered by a man named Woodruff who worked in sales at the Neil Motor Company in Willmar, Minnesota. Al already had a strong working relationship with the Neil's and had been selling cars for them for nearly two years.

Al never had more than two cars on his lot at any one time. This car was different, probably the most nicely appointed traveling machine in Grant County. This Chrysler had been previously owned by a high executive in the General Mills Corporation in Minneapolis. It not only looked nice but had a classic past. Although most people in the area could not afford such a car, Al fell in love with the vehicle and decided to take a chance. This was an opportunity to advance the image of his rapidly developing business in the County.

He invited his soon-to-be wife, Myrtle Gieselman, from Morris to examine this beautiful automobile. They dreamed that the commission from selling this vehicle would pay all their wedding expenses when they married in June. It seems that everyone in Herman knew that something special was happening for Al. Merrit Watson even took a walk from his small filling station to examine this jewel of a car. He was a very heavy man, so the trip required effort.

Wayne Hartman had to pass the small car lot every time he went to see his mother. He always examined the automobiles that Al had for sale. On this day, he saw the beautiful, shiny Chrysler sitting handsomely on the lot. With excitement, he slammed on the brakes and turned his car into Schreader's business. The car door to this beauty was locked, so Wayne went into the building to ask Al Schreader if he could drive the car.

Schreader responded with a quick, "No."

He was sure that Hartman did not have the money and that Hartman planned to drive the car around the area until he was forced to give it up. He had done that with other cars, so by this time, most folks were quite aware of Wayne's deceptive practices.

Wayne and Sara sat in the old Model A and dreamed

about how wonderful life could be if only they owned such a car. Sara knew that they might never be able to own a car with such luxury. However, she indulged Wayne in the fantasy filled dream.

They drove past the car several times on their way to Slim Watson's filling station. Sara had one dollar in her purse, so she offered to pay for the eight gallons of gasoline. While Wayne waited for Meritt Watson to put in the eight gallons of gas, he gazed across the street at the "Bloody Bucket." It was the local pub that hosted many people his age.

He really wanted to feel accepted and admired by these young men. The young men of the community saw him as a person who was weak and untrustworthy.

Wayne got into his car with Sara and retraced the two blocks back to Al Schreader's filling station. He slowly opened the door of his car and walked toward the shiny Chrysler. Al noticed that Wayne was again looking at the car.

He set aside his tools and went outside to talk to Hartman. Wayne made some small talk and again asked to drive the car. Again, Schreader stiffly refused. Woodruff, the salesman from the Neil Motor Company of Wilmer, joined the two men by the car. The conversation between Schreader and Hartman was tense since Schreader had already refused Hartman's request to drive the car on four separate occasions.

With his head hanging, Hartman joined Sara in their old car. They returned to the farm home with little conversation. The evening was filled with tension. However, as the evening wore on, Wayne's mood began to improve. Norma noticed the improvement but did not dare to ask about the change.

Throughout much of the evening Wayne had cursed and mumbled under his breath with threats toward Schreader and Woodruff. Wayne just had to have that car! There simply was no alternative.

His mood improved because he had devised a plan to get the car. He decided that they would travel to Elbow Lake in the morning and ask his mother for five hundred dollars. Prior to this, she had only lent him seventy-five dollars to purchase harnesses for the horses. The other money she had given Wayne to buy groceries and other necessities amounted to less than ten dollars each time.

Wayne's hopes were high and he focused all of his attention on this new plan. This is all he could think about. He came to bed at two AM and fell asleep quickly. He had decided that he could buy the car with his mother's money instead of just driving it around until he was forced to return it.

He had visions of driving it down the streets of Herman with people saying, "Wayne, your car is beautiful, you are such an impressive guy."

CHAPTER 23

THE PLAN

WAYNE WAS UP EARLY THE FOLLOWING MORNING filled with excitement and anticipation. His drastically changed behaviors confused Sara because he seldom showed any enthusiasm in the morning. She knew better than to ask Wayne what he was thinking. His answers were usually convoluted and misleading, so she never learned anything by asking him anyway. She felt tension but went no further with inquiries into his changed mood.

He said, "Get your coat, we are going to Elbow Lake to see my mother."

During the thirty-minute drive, he only spoke of owning that Chrysler and how his life would change for the better once he owned that car. He just knew that his mother would give him the money. He was nervous and excited and never considered the possibility that she might refuse. Sometime around 11:00 AM they arrived at the Flint home. He jumped from the car without waiting for Sara and rushed into the house.

Before saying hello to either Ada or Morris, he said, "Mom, I need five hundred dollars today." The demand shocked her.

She asked, "Why in heavens name do you need that large amount of money?"

Wayne responded matter-of-factly, "I have found a car that I want to buy, and I want to borrow the money from you. I will pay you back."

Ada had heard Wayne say he would pay back money he had borrowed from her before many times. He had never paid her back any money that he had borrowed. This was much more than he had ever asked for before. She could not imagine that this time would be any different. The only difference was the amount of money he was asking from her. The short tense interaction ended abruptly when she refused to give him the money.

Wayne angrily left the house, slammed the door and ordered Sara into the car. She was frightened. The drive back to the farm was fast and without conversation. Wayne had never hit Sara but she did feel that if there was first time, this was it.

Arriving at the farm, he stopped the car, and he and Sara went into the house. Wayne refused to speak. The rest of the day passed in silence. That evening Sara went to bed while Wayne sat in the living room chair staring straight ahead out the window, brooding. Sara slept poorly and awakened early. Wayne was still sitting in the living room staring out the window.

He said, "I am planning to go to town in a little while. You can stay home and fix dinner."

His affect had changed completely from the night before. He was again confident and focused. This was just another mood change that confused Sara. She was glad he did not want her to join him in his trip to town.

Wayne left the house and got into his old Model A Ford. The small four-cylinder engine resisted slightly before beginning to move on its way to Herman.

The Plan

The air was chilly on this late March morning. The trip took Wayne past the Schreader garage with the shiny Chrysler. This time he traveled on to the Herman Co-Op Elevator. He had another plan that he was sure would get him the Chrysler.

He opened the dusty windowed door of the elevator and stepped onto the warn wooden floor. He did not recognize anyone nor did anyone respond to him. If any of the men standing around recognized him, they quickly looked away. No one wanted to be approached by Wayne Hartman.

Walking to the counter, he smiled sweetly at the clerk and said, "I would like to have a counter check for the Herman National Bank."

The feed salesman reached down to the packs of counter checks and set six packs of checks from area banks on the counter. The ones from the Herman National Bank were light blue.

Wayne said, "I need four."

Without question, the feed salesman reached across the counter and handed Wayne his requested four checks. Wayne had never used a counter check before, but he had seen his stepfather and his uncle Ray use them. Folks often used counter checks to pay for items when they left their own check book at home. Local merchants accepted these counter checks as readily as cash in exchange for various materials from groceries to large pieces of farm machinery.

Wayne had never noticed what was on these pieces of paper, but did notice that the recipient of the check usually filled it out. He was sure that if he offered one of these pieces of paper to Al Schreader and had him fill it out, he would then receive the car. His problems seemed to be solved.

Leaving the grain elevator with the dusty floors and

windows, Wayne got into his car, started the engine and drove toward the Schreader garage. He parked his car near the side of the building and opened the door to begin his venture into the building where he felt the sale would take place.

Schreader was working in his office with Mr. Woodruff. They slowly looked up and gazed at Hartman. They did not get up from their chairs. They assumed that he was again going to apply pressure on them to allow him to drive the shiny Chrysler.

Hartman went to the open office door and confidently said, "I would like to purchase the Chrysler."

The room fell silent.

Schreader responded, "The price is $488, do you have the money?"

Hartman reached into his pocket for his billfold and clumsily withdrew one of the light blue counter checks. Schreader looked with amazement and took the piece of paper from Hartman.

He then asked, "What do you think your car is worth?"

Hartman was confused and didn't respond.

Schreader said, "I will give you $50 for the car, you will then owe me $438."

Not being sure of what had just happened, Hartman responded, "OK."

The check was completed by Schreader and handed to Hartman for signature. Not realizing that a signature was required, Hartman clumsily signed his name. The deal was done. State government papers were also signed. Schreader stood and shook Hartman's hand. Hartman smiled and accepted the keys. Hartman handed Schreader the keys to his Model A.

The Plan

With a million-dollar smile Hartman excitedly walked to the Chrysler. This new car was his dream!

Even though the car was nearly full of gas, Hartman drove to Slim Watson's filling station across the street from the Bloody Bucket.

Slim got up from his chair with a beaming smile and said, "Wow, what a beauty, whose is it?"

Hartman beamed in triumph and said, "It's mine."

Unfortunately, there was no one standing in front of the Bloody Bucket to admire Wayne with his new car.

Disappointed that there was no one to admire his beautiful car except Slim Watson, Hartman started to drive the eight miles toward his home. He was sure that Sara would like the car and would be excited to go for a ride.

Arriving at the farm, he went into the house and told Sara to look out the window. After seeing the shiny Chrysler in front of their house, she jumped up and gave Wayne a big hug.

He said, "I would like to go to Elbow Lake to show it to my mother and Morris."

They ate lunch and readied themselves for the trip. Wayne continuously talked for the whole trip about how excited people would be to see him in the new car. He had never felt more fulfilled and he loved it.

Arriving at his mother's home, he ran to the house so excited to see her smile. Without knocking he entered the house and excitedly demanded that she immediately come to the window. She obeyed her eager son and did what he asked. Sara stood by the car with a look of joy on her face as she waited for Ada and Morris to gaze with admiration at Wayne's new car.

Morris was puzzled by all the commotion, so he hesitated to approach the window. Wayne's younger brother and sister paid little attention and refused to move in that direction. As Ada approached the window she caught a glimpse of the new car.

"How did you get that?" Her voice held no joy, only surprise and confusion. She dreaded Wayne's answer. Wayne smiled broadly without reacting to his mother's voice that choked a controlled panic.

He said, "I bought it this morning. It's mine. I now have the nicest car in the area."

Morris joined Ada at the window. His face was expressionless and hers was filled with dismay and shock as they stared at the new Chrysler.

She could only think the worst when she said, "You don't have that kind of money. You can't afford that car. What have you done?"

Without much expression, Wayne happily said, "I paid for it with a check, I've seen dad do it many times."

Ada screamed, "You have no money in the bank. You have to have money in a bank account in order to write checks. The police will arrest you and put you in jail. Oh my God, Wayne, writing checks on a bank without money is against the law."

Wayne looked puzzled. Wayne's mother's anger only confused him. He could tell that the light blue check was a cause for trouble, but he did not completely understand why that was such a problem. As was typical, Wayne withdrew into himself and did not respond to the threats and noises that were being hurled about the room.

Sara knew that something bad had happened when no one came out of the house to admire their new car. She walked into the house to a firestorm of breathless confusion and anger. Everyone hurling insults and abuse at each other. Wayne stormed out of the house leaving Sara speechless. He briskly walked to his new car and left without her.

By now Ada's face was filled with tears. Tears were also on Sara's cheeks. Both women realized the trouble that Wayne was now in.

Wayne drove at a steady pace back to the farm. He reasoned that his mother's fears were serious. He then figured that if he got the check back, there would no longer be a problem. He also concluded that if he could somehow get the check back, he could still keep the car.

As he passed the Schreader car sales lot, he thought that if he had some repair work done on the car like new tires and gave Schreader another check for $538.40, the old check would be returned. This would then solve the problem of the first check that made Ada so upset. He still failed to make an association between the check and having money in the bank to cover the check.

Later that evening Morris and Ada drove Sara back home. They discovered that there was now a new and larger check in Schreader's hands. Wayne had explained to them how he had cleverly solved the problem of the first check. Again, Ada began to scream and cry while trying to explain to Wayne that he had broken the law in a serious way.

The only thing that made any sense to Wayne was that he must get the new check back from Al Schreader. It never occurred to him to give up the car. That was the focal point of his dreams and nothing was going to take it away.

CHAPTER 24

THE BAD CHECK

THE NEXT DAY, SCHREADER'S AFTERNOON was very busy repairing automobiles, but he had just enough time to deposit Wayne's check before the bank closed at 3:00 PM. He told his shop employee, Vernon Easley, that he was going to the bank to deposit the check into the Neil Motor Company account. He said he was also going to retain the $53.84 for his account as the commission for selling the car. Additionally, there was an uncertain profit for the tires. But the Neil Motor Company would settle with him later as they had done in the past. That settlement would also be added to initial commission to be put into the wedding account for him and Myrtle.

This was a very good day. He had retained earnings of nearly one hundred dollars. He kept twenty dollars in the cash register for his drive to Morris and a date with Myrtle. They planned an evening meal at the Delmonico café and a movie at the Morris Theatre. Things had never looked better.

With a spring in his step, he walked the one block to the Herman National Bank. He was greeted by the regular teller, Eleanor. He liked seeing her. She was always friendly and sometimes flirted even though he knew she was married and had four children.

At the teller's window, Al placed the light blue piece of

paper on the counter. Still smiling Eleanor dropped her eyes to the check and asked Al how the deposit should be made. Upon examination, her eyes changed from smiling to puzzled.

She said, "This person does not have an account at our bank. There is nothing I can do."

She knew that the matter was serious. Al's face turned from smiling and confident to dizzy.

"Oh, my God," he cried. There was nothing he could do. He had just given a man a very expensive automobile and received nothing. The planned events for the evening simply disappeared. His wedding savings evaporated as he clutched the worthless piece of paper. His heart raced. How would he explain this mess? How would he get the car back? Should he call the police?

He turned from the friendly teller and almost ran to the door. His heart was pounding and his breathing was deep. The rage was beginning to build. He knew now that he had been deceived. Half crying and gasping he looked for Woodruff. This meant trouble for both of them. What to do? Finding Woodruff in the back of the building readying himself for a late afternoon trip to Willmar, he explained what had happened. He was embarrassed and ashamed. He barely knew Wayne Hartman and still accepted a check from him for the car. He never dreamt that anyone would write a bad check in Herman, Minnesota.

With anxiety and embarrassment, the two men reviewed the facts of their situation. They decided to drive to the Hartman farm despite the difficulty of finding it in the dark. Stopping by several farms on the trip they eventually arrived at their destination. They knocked. Sara, not knowing them, greeted the two men with surprise. They asked for her husband. She called and he got up from the table leaving his evening meal behind and came to the door.

The men attempted to maintain their composure stating that there was no money in the bank to cover the check Wayne had written. Hartman not realizing that there was supposed to be money covering each transaction reacted somewhat bewildered. His mother's fears from her earlier shouts now started to make sense.

No one seemed sure of what the next step might be. Hartman began to think that he had a solution for this tense situation. He suggested that they join him to drive to Elbow Lake to talk to Ada's husband, Morris. Wayne acted as if he was sure that his stepfather would supply them with the money to cover the check, so that he could keep the car. A tense interchange followed.

Al and Woodruff finally agreed that they would leave the car and return in the morning for the trip to Elbow Lake. Wayne knew that he needed to get the check if he was to keep the car. His mind was beginning to formulate a plan.

CHAPTER 25

A NEW PLAN

WAYNE SLEPT RESTLESSLY THAT NIGHT and awoke early. His plan was clear in his mind. He had three pieces of chocolate candy left over from the Easter holiday. He also had a product in the house called "Rough-On-Rats." The product was sold at the local elevator and was used in barnyards infested with rats. It was a derivative of strychnine. Wayne placed a small amount into the pieces of candy making sure there was at least one piece that he could eat which was free of the poison.

Al and Woodruff arrived promptly at the Hartman farm at 9:30 AM to travel to Alexandria where they would meet with Wayne's stepfather. They knew that Morris was a cattleman and had heard that he had just sold a small herd so had substantial cash with which to buy the car. Things seemed to be looking up for Al and Woodruff. They had no idea that Wayne had already asked to borrow the money for the car and been refused.

There was still a tinge of frost in the air as the three tense men got into the shiny new Chrysler and headed for Alexandria. Al sat in the front seat with Hartman. Woodruff sat directly behind Al. As they approached Hoffman on Highway twenty-seven, Hartman reached in his pocket offering each man a piece of chocolate candy. He saved one for himself and began eating. The other two men followed his lead and began to eat.

Immediately the bitterness of the strychnine hit their tongue. Al immediately spit the bitter tasting candy on the floor, but Woodruff chose to swallow it instead. Shortly afterward, he began to scream and choke and showed signs of convulsing and dying.

Al demanded that Hartman drive immediately to the Alexandria Hospital. Rushing into the open door with Woodruff's arms over their shoulders, the three men were met by Dr. Hans Peterson of the medical staff. Woodruff's pulse was uneven, but he was alive.

Liquid drained from his mouth as he lay in the emergency room. A nurse came into the room to get a sample to take to the lab in Minneapolis for analysis. Both the doctor and the nurse believed that they were seeing the effects of a disease. Dramatic illnesses with rapid onsets were somewhat common in those times. They feared that this new disease might infect others. Caution and speed were of the essence.

A sheriff's deputy was immediately sent with the sample to the University of Minnesota Hospital for a laboratory analysis. This would take the better part of the day since the University was about one hundred and forty miles away. Dr. Peterson, Al Schreader and the hospital staff were on edge. It was not clear whether or not Woodruff would survive this acute disease onset.

No one seemed to notice that Wayne Hartman stood by the waiting room quite relaxed. Thinking that Woodruff might die, Schreader allowed the day to pass out of respect for his seriously ill partner. He also thought that he might begin to experience the same symptoms as Woodruff if the disease were contagious. The drive back to Herman was quiet. Neither Al nor Wayne spoke except to arrange for another trip to Alexandria to get the money for the car from Morris.

Arriving back at his home, Hartman ignored Sara's many questions.

He then picked up his 22-caliber rifle and said, "Find me the shells. I am going hunting."

Sara handed Wayne a full box of shells. He took only three. She asked, "Why not take the box?"

Wayne responded, "Three will be enough. The flyways are filled with ducks and geese, so it will be easy to get enough for us."

Hartman left the house in the shiny Chrysler. On his way he stopped and loaded the rifle. He also had an old binder canvas that he used for wrapping the gun. He placed the canvas over the gun in the back seat of the Chrysler and drove toward Donnelly. About a half mile from Donnelly, he allowed the car to slide from the road. He was close to the village liquor store where he knew there was a phone. After walking to the store, he called for Schreader to come and extract the car from the ditch. However, Al was not in the building when the phone rang, so Wayne left his message with Vernon Easley, Schreader's hired man. Hartman returned to the car and waited for Al Schreader to come after receiving the message from Vernon.

Several hours passed but Schreader had not yet come. With each passing hour Hartman's anxiety grew. He had to get the check back. It seemed to him that getting the check would somehow release him from all responsibility and still allow him to keep the car.

Finally, he gave up waiting for Al, so he removed the car from the ditch himself and headed back to his house. To Sara he appeared anxious for the first time in a long time. He did not share with her any of the events of that day.

As evening approached, he said, "I am going outside to feed the hogs."

Instead of immediately feeding the animals, he went to the barn and found a large unattached door that was leaning against the wall. He pulled the door into the hog barn from the pen. Then he got a shovel and began to dig a hole in the hog barn. While he was busily working on digging the hole deeper, some friends arrived and asked what he was doing.

Startled he responded, "I am digging a hole for the rats that are dying around the barn and hog pen. This is the only place where the ground is not frozen and it's possible for me to dig. I am planning to put cement on this floor in the Spring."

The idea seemed reasonable, so the folks stayed around and visited for a while. After they left, he finished digging the hole in the hog barn. He put the barn door over the hole and spread the straw bedding over the door. That made the hole in the floor of the barn invisible to anyone entering the hog barn. After he fed the animals, he calmly returned to the house.

It was dark. Sara had already eaten. Wayne sat and ate his cold meal without uttering a word to Sara.

Afterwards he went to the living room and stared out the window into the darkness. He was expressionless and did not respond to any of Sara's comments. The night passed with Wayne remaining in the chair, still expressionless. Sara got up in the morning to find Wayne in the same spot in the living room, still staring out the window.

She offered a "Good morning" but he said nothing in return.

She fixed breakfast and tried to start a conversation to no avail.

A New Plan

Schreader arrived at the Hartman farm midmorning to begin another trip to Alexandria in an effort to get the money. Hartman had assured him that his stepfather would settle the bill with cash. With each manipulation, Schreader grew angrier. By this time, he had developed a deep hatred for the man who seemed to be continuously making excuses.

Hartman's determination to keep the shiny Chrysler grew more intense. Again, the car was started as the two men left the farm with Wayne driving. They passed through Herman and onto Highway twenty-seven headed to Alexandria. Few words were spoken.

About five miles past Herman near Ristow Woods, Hartman said, "There is something wrong with the left rear tire, I feel it shake."

He pulled the car over on a path adjacent to a large grove of trees and got out to look. Schreader also got out of the car and walked around the rear to examine the tire. As Schreader headed for the tire, Hartman went to the passenger door and removed the rifle from the binder canvas.

Schreader could not understand why there would be a problem with the tire since all the tires were new. He got down on his knees to examine the tire more closely. He felt around the tire and could find no fault. As he continued to look at the tire, he began to explain to Hartman that he couldn't find anything wrong with it. Meanwhile, Hartman pointed the rifle at the back of Schreader's head and pulled the trigger. Schreader jerked and stiffened slowly falling on his side.

After the explosion of the rifle, all was quiet.

Hartman pulled the billfold from Schreader's pocket and found the check that he was convinced had caused all the problems for him. He left the money and again opened Schreader's pocket to return the wallet.

Without emotion, Hartman lifted the dead body into the now open trunk and slammed it shut. He returned the rifle to the rear seat of the car with one expended shell. However, he was not sure what to do next. He started the car, backed out of the woods and headed for Fahlstrand Corner. There he waited until turning the car around and again traveling past the site of the murder and on to County Road Eighteen toward Norcross.

Several miles past Highway Twenty-Seven, Hartman pulled to the side of the road. He got out of the car, opened the passenger door and then opened the trunk. Momentarily he gazed at the dead body and considered his predicament. He reached into the trunk placing one arm under the already stiffening arm and the other around the shoulder. Lifting the dead body from the trunk, he carried it to the passenger door and sat it upright in the passenger seat. The neck had not yet stiffened and as a result it bent to the side and just over the back.

Hartman stepped back from the door and closed it. Walking to the open trunk he noticed a tiny pool of blood. Slamming the trunk door, he went to the driver seat to sit beside the Al Schreader's body. Again, without panic, Hartman calmly drove along the gravel road and into the village of Norcross. The Main Street was empty. There was no one to notice the shiny Chrysler.

In late March darkness arrives around 6:30 PM. It was shortly after that when he drove into his own farmyard. He calmly walked into the house and shared an evening meal with Sara. She could not detect any mood change as he sat there eating.

Finishing his meal, he said, "I am going out to feed the pigs. It will take about a half hour."

Leaving the house, he got into the Chrysler with the dead body at his side. It was now very dark. He drove the car between the large pile of straw and the opening to the hog pen. He went into the pen and removed the straw and large door over the hole. He went back to the car and dragged Al Schreader's body from the passenger side of the car. Placing his arms under both of Schreader's arms, he dragged it through the animal waste and dropped it in the hole. He then replaced the door and spread animal waste over it.

He could hear the confused pigs noisily grunting in the yard. Their night vision is poor, so they were not able to detect what was disrupting their space. He could also hear rats scurrying along the rafters and two by fours of the barn. He knew the rats would soon burrow their way into the manure and find the dead flesh on which to feast.

Returning to the house, he had a short conversation with Sara and went to bed for a good night's sleep. He was relieved to know he had the check. Could his problems be over?

The next morning Sara said, "I would like to go to town and get some groceries. Our parents are coming to visit this afternoon."

Midmorning they drove the car for the short journey to town. Sara immediately noticed that there were dark stains on the top of the passenger seat. She questioned Wayne as to why his new vehicle already had a serious blemish on the seat.

Without affect, Hartman said, "That is from the goose that I shot yesterday."

In Sara's mind all seemed in order and properly explained.

CHAPTER 26

THE SEARCH

By now, people were beginning to miss Al Schreader. Vern Esterley, Al's hired man, went to talk to Sheriff Amundsen to share his concern about Al. He explained that it was not like Al to be late to work let alone not come at all the previous day.

Myrtle Gieselmen, his finance, had been stood up on her date for a dinner and movie. This was not like Al to leave her standing, so she contacted Al's parents sharing her concern and hoping for a satisfactory explanation. The Sheriff organized his deputies and some townsfolk to begin a serious search that Sunday morning. There was no obvious explanation for Al's disappearance.

On Sunday, April 2, 1939, Ed Schreader, Al's brother, went to Al Winkles' house in Morris, Minnesota, to ask if he would like to ride with him to Herman. It was Sunday afternoon. Ed told him that his brother, Al, was missing and had not been heard from since Saturday.

Ed told Winkles that his brother, Al, was to have gone to his parents' farm near Alberta on Sunday. He never arrived. Ed repeated what he had heard earlier that Al had left Herman on Saturday afternoon with someone. Apparently, he had just sold a car to this unknown man. He never returned to his business in Herman on Saturday night.

People who knew Al were getting concerned and worried as to what might have happened. Winkels got in the car with Ed and traveled the eighteen miles to Herman. When the two men arrived in Herman, Vern Esterly, a mechanic at Al's garage, and Deputy Cory were at already there trying to decide what to do. While discussing options with the new arrivals, Bill Schreader and Francis Gieselman arrived from Alberta and Chokio. Bill Schreader was Al and Ed's uncle. Francis Gieselman was a brother-in-law.

Vern told the group that Al was going to Alexandia with a man named Wayne Hartman to get some money to cover a check Wayne had written for the car. As soon as they heard that the unknown man was Wayne Hartman they became concerned because they knew that he was "different."

The men decided that questioning Wayne about the disappearance of Al was the tactic that they needed to pursue. They hatched a plan to get Wayne to come into Grant County under the pretense of discussing the situation with the car. Wayne's farm was located in Traverse County, so the officials in Grant County did not have jurisdiction. They had to lure him into Grant County, so they could question him. Once he was in Herman at the garage, which is in Grant County, they would question him about Al's disappearance.

Vern Esterly and Ed Schreader went to the Hartman farm and asked Wayne to come to town. They suggested that they needed him to clear up the issues surrounding the car. They would not tell him that he was their primary suspect regarding the disappearance of Al Schreader.

After some discussion, Hartman agreed to drive his shiny Chrysler which he had "purchased" from Al back to Herman. After convincing Wayne to return to Herman, Vern and Ed got back into their car and drove back to the garage.

On the way, they hit a pheasant which broke their windshield. Hartman followed them a short time later.

When they arrived at the garage, the deputy sheriff was waiting. He took Hartman in the back room and questioned him with no results. After expressing frustration with the lack of progress in the questioning of Wayne, the Deputy called Sheriff Amundson. He arrived to further question Hartman who offered several stories regarding Al's disappearance.

Wayne looked into the Sheriff's eyes and said, "You have nothing on me."

With the many conflicting stories Wayne told them, the sheriff and deputy decided to take Hartman back to Barrett in an effort to verify his alibis.

The other men also wanted to go, so the Sheriff assented. He told the others, "You can follow us in another car."

The Sheriff, his deputy and Vern Esterly rode in the lead vehicle with Wayne Hartman. Ed Schreader, Bill Schreader, Francis Gieselman and Winkels rode in the second automobile. They traveled to Barrett and went to the restaurant where Wayne said that he and Al had eaten lunch to ask if anyone there had seen or heard of Wayne Hartman. No one remembered seeing Wayne or Al.

From Barrett they went to Alexandria to meet with Morris Flint, Wayne Hartman's stepfather. He was rather rude and not cooperative, but did not verify any of Hartman's stories. The men were stumped. They were a group of people from Grant County in Douglas County with a suspect and no evidence.

Sheriff Amundson decided to remain in Alexandria and take Hartman to the Douglas County Sheriff's office. The Douglas County Sheriff lived near the county jail, so Sheriff Amundson went to his house to ask for help.

CHAPTER 27

THE CONFESSION

THE DOUGLAS COUNTY SHERIFF TOOK HARTMAN into an interrogation room with several other Deputies. Hartman usually withdrew in times of crisis and again used that technique. He refused to look at the Sheriff and said nothing throughout the attempt to question him.

One of the interrogators from Douglas County had been a successful Golden Gloves boxer and had his own method for interrogation. In spite of it all, Hartman remained silent. The interrogation continued. When the Deputy emerged from the interrogation with the Sheriff, there was blood on his clothing. The Deputy explained that the blood was from killing chickens the other day when he was off duty.

After a short break, they returned to the interrogation room. Similar methods were used, and after a short time, Wayne Hartman confessed that he had killed Al Schreader. He acknowledged the deed by signing several forms. When the interrogators asked him where they could find the body, Wayne again remained silent. The interrogation continued. Finally, sometime after midnight, Hartman revealed the body's location. It was in the hog barn.

Because it was late and they decided to keep Hartman in the Douglas County jail. The Grant County Sheriff, Deputy and other folks piled into the two automobiles and left Alexandria to head for the Hartman farm in Traverse County, Minnesota, where Wayne had said he had buried Al's body. The date was April 3, 1939.

Arriving at the farm, Sheriff Amundson went to the house and knocked on the door, but no one answered his knock. He entered the house to call for Sara and saw the rifle leaning against the wall in the kitchen with two remaining shells.

The group immediately went to the hog barn and chased the pigs outside into a large pen. Because it was still dark, they used flashlights as they probed the manure with pitchforks trying to find Al's body. After unsuccessfully searching for an hour, they were about to give up.

One of the deputies said, "Let's go. I think he sent us on a wild goose chase."

Deputy Cory was more determined. He took a fork and systematically covered the whole area again. Finally, he hit a spot where the door was covering the body.

He said, "I think it's here."

They began to clean the straw and manure from the wood door. They raised the door and there in the shallow grave lay the body of Al Schreader. They lifted the body from the grave and rolled him on his back where they found that he had been shot one time in the back of the head.

It was a pitch-black night with no moon or stars visible. They only had two flashlights which both belonged to Sheriff Amundson. The Hartman farm had no phone so Sheriff Amundson needed to drive back to Herman to notify the Traverse County Sheriff and coroner that they had just found a body.

The Sheriff climbed into his car with his Deputies to go back to Herman. He left Bill Schreader and Francis Geiselman behind to protect the body from the hogs. These two men were nervous because it was totally dark, and they didn't have a flashlight.

The Deputies teased them about being scared but finally left one of the flashlights with them. Even with the flashlight, the two men that remained were very uneasy in the dark hog house with the dead body.

The news of Al's discovery quickly spread to family members. Martin and Martha, Al's parents, were told of the shocking news Monday morning. They sat and cried while questioning the people who arrived with the news. They realized that once again they would have to prepare for a funeral and a burial.

After some time their other children joined them, the family reflected on the loss of their sister and oldest daughter, Elizabeth, who had died as a result of the difficult journey they had taken from Germany.

Martha listened to the sad conversation and slowly got up from the living room couch and went to her bedroom. She made no comment. People looked up as she left the room, they offered no questions. Slowly Martha walked to a chest of drawers that she used for her clothing. She opened one of the doors and slid the clothes aside as she peered at the Colt 45. She had not looked at it in years. She needed to reassure herself that it was still there and ready for use if she needed it to ensure justice for her son, Al. Covering the gun, she walked back into the living room and sat down.

Another nightmare had struck her life.

Al's funeral was scheduled for the Assumption Church in Morris with Monsignor Fearon officiating. Myrtle Geiselman, Al's fiancée, and his mother, Martha, followed directly behind the casket into the church with Martin slightly behind. The church service was rather long with many mourners in attendance. Monsignor Fearon gave a lengthy eulogy. After the service, the group made their way to the Assumption Cemetery where Al Schreader was laid to rest.

CHAPTER 28

THE TRIAL AND SENTENCE

COURT PROCEEDINGS BEGAN PROMPTLY. They would last until the final sentencing done in late June 1939.

During the sentencing hearing, the court took testimony from community members. Myrtle Geiselman, Al's fiancee, sat with Al's suffering mother, Martha. Across the courtroom was another suffering woman, Ada Flint, Wayne Hartman's mother.

Wayne Hartman was found guilty of first-degree premeditated murder and sentenced to life behind bars at the state penitentiary in Stillwater, Minnesota. Afterwards, Judge Flaherty sounded his gavel adjourning the court.

Cautiously observing each other, the three women moved toward each other and then hugged with a flood of tears. For two of them the nightmare was over with only memories. But Ada would live with the disaster throughout the remainder of her life.

On June 29, 1939, Wayne Hartman left the Grant County Courthouse in Elbow Lake, Minnesota, and climbed into the deputy sheriff's automobile for his ride to the state penitentiary in Stillwater. He had just been sentenced to life in prison for the murder of Aloysius Schreader.

EPILOGUE

Wayne's many years in that prison revealed a human being who adapted well to prison life. He committed no violent acts in Stillwater during the nearly 30 years of his incarceration. Although he made requests for release approximately every three years, he always accepted the parole board's recommendation for continuation of his sentence.

Early during his incarceration, he became the head prison butcher because of his experience with his hogs. He remained in that capacity for nearly 30 years.

His mother, Ada, never once suggested her son was innocent. She remained loyal to him and visited regularly.

After multiple appeals failed, he was finally granted release on November 22, 1966. Afterwards, he boarded a plane to Bakersfield, California, to work for his brother.

After working for his brother for one year, he opened a convalescent home for the elderly and was licensed by the State of California to do such work.

Ada and her husband, Morris Flint, moved to Bakersfield to be with Wayne and his brother immediately after Wayne's release. She remained with them through the remainder of her life.

Wayne Hartman died May 12, 1968, of a sudden heart attack.

The people of West Central Minnesota had come to describe this man as a vicious killer who operated far outside the law. It was not until his twenty-eight-year record in Stillwater prison was revealed that people in the area surrounding Grant County understood that Wayne's basic nature was passive.

This revelation was in stark contrast to the impressions and opinions of people who thought they knew him. Wayne Hartman received a psychiatric evaluation every three years. All psychological and psychiatric evaluations noted that he felt no regret regarding the murder. His emotions were apathetic regarding killing Al Schreader.

It was not until 1965 that a psychiatrist evaluated him and gave him a diagnosis of a schizoid personality disorder.

The following is a summary of that diagnostic impression:

The essential feature of a schizoid personality is a pervasive pattern of detachment from social relationships and a restricted range of expression of emotion in interpersonal settings. They are indifferent to close relationships and do not seem to derive much satisfaction from being part of a family. They would rather be alone than with others. They show emotional coldness and detachment and are very rarely sexually intimate. They are indifferent to praise and criticism from others. These features as they are understood today were far from the spectrum of understanding in 1939. People with this disorder today are helped to restructure their lives in an effort to find a place of comfort. The basic pattern of adjustment is ongoing, often frustrating the concerns of people who care for them.

Sara divorced Wayne after he confessed to the murder and made no attempt to contact him after that. They had been married only three months at the time of the murder. Sara did relate her experience on the day of the murder to the court. She indicated that Wayne had dropped her off in

Herman on Saturday evening to do some shopping. Stores were usually open in small towns such as Herman on Saturday evenings, and she was to meet him at the Schreader service station after Wayne and Al returned from their trip to Alexandria.

He did not return that evening at the agreed upon time to pick up Sara so she went to her parent's home. By this time, Schreader was no longer alive. Hartman realized he had to pick up his wife, so he returned the body to the trunk before picking her up and returning to their farm.

Sara indicated that she did not notice anything out of the ordinary when she climbed into the car. She said she was angry with him leaving her so long, so she was upset and did not see anything that would indicate that something had happened to Al.

The search for Al Scherader was written in a letter many years later by Mr. Winkels. He wrote in his recounting of the events that whoever is interested in reading the articles from the newspapers and court records, will find discrepancies. The facts told in his letter are as he remembered them. The newspaper articles are interesting and thorough, but many of the details are missing so people who are interested in the details surrounding the murder will not have a complete picture.

In his letter Winkles says, "At this time I am the only living person left from those days. I know firsthand the details of that eventful time."

ACKNOWLEDGEMENTS

The power of curiosity leads us in our efforts to understand things and events that surround us. I am grateful to the many individuals who told stories about people and events throughout my childhood. This book is a reflection of one of those stories told by many of the adults that surrounded me when I was a child.

I am grateful to Don Geiselmann who lives in the area where the crime took place. He spent time talking to relatives of people connected to the events of that time in order to help me gain perspective. We then spent hours discussing the various players and personalities associated with Wayne Hartman and Al Schreader.

I am thankful that the Minnesota State Penitentiary was so gracious in furnishing me the files they had on Wayne Hartman and to the courthouse and newspaper archives which helped me develop the events of that time.

Thanks to Janet Lawson who helped me polish my ideas and for giving me support and encouragement.

Most of all, I thank my wife, Karen, who edited my work numerous times and offered advice and encouragement. Words could never thank her enough.

SIMON ZELLER grew up in the least populated county in western Minnesota. He was born in a family home without running water or a telephone. He graduated from Wheaton High School and went on to the University of Minnesota, Morris. After completing his service in the military in the Republic of Korea, he attended the University of Missouri in Columbia receiving a Master's Degree in Social Work. He worked nearly fifty years in the field of social work primarily with chronic psychiatric patients. Simon and his wife, Karen, have five children and eight grandchildren. They live in Faribault, Minnesota, among children and grandchildren who are an everyday part of their lives. He has published one other book, *Think About This*, which focuses on the practice of social work.